PRAISE FOR WILLIAM SHATNER AND HIS ELECTRIFYING *TEK* NOVELS . . .

TEKWAR

Introducing Jake Cardigan, a tough ex-cop battling a world of high-tech drugs and future shock . . .

"FAST-PACED SF ACTION ADVENTURE!"

—*Library Journal*

"SHATNER DELIVERS . . . THE PACE IS UNRELENTING!" —*Publishers Weekly*

TEKLORDS

Jake Cardigan fights reprogrammed human "zombies" to pierce the powerful heart of the TekLords . . .

"A COMBINATION OF *MIAMI VICE* AND *BLADE RUNNER*." —*Locus*

TEKLAB

The ruins of twenty-first century London are the battleground for Jake Cardigan and a deadly serial killer . . .

"SHATNER IS A GOOD WRITER . . . THIS READER AWAITS HIS NEXT EFFORT!"

—*Nashville Banner*

TEK VENGEANCE

The murder of Cardigan's girlfriend is the worst mistake the TekLords could have made . . .

"FAST ACTION . . . TONGUE-IN-CHEEK HUMOR . . . A GOOD READ!" —*Booklist*

Ace Books by William Shatner

TEKWAR
TEKLORDS
TEKLAB
TEK VENGEANCE
TEK SECRET

TEK SECRET

WILLIAM SHATNER

ACE BOOKS, NEW YORK

This Ace Book contains the complete text of the original hardcover edition. It has been completely reset in a typeface designed for easy reading, and was printed from new film.

TEK SECRET

An Ace Book / published by arrangement with
the author

PRINTING HISTORY
Ace / Putnam hardcover edition published 1993
Ace paperback edition / December 1994

Cover art by Boris Vallejo.

ISBN: 0-441-00119-X

ACE®
Ace Books are published by The Berkley Publishing Group,
200 Madison Avenue, New York, New York 10016.
ACE and the "A" design are trademarks
belonging to Charter Communications, Inc.

PRINTED IN THE UNITED STATES OF AMERICA

10 9 8 7 6 5 4 3 2 1

During the intervening months between *Tek Vengeance* and this book, I had the opportunity to meet a group of dedicated professionals who are consumed with making the movie *cum* series, *TekWar.*

They are many in number and varied in skill. They range from the caterer to the cinematographer to the producers to the script supervisor and all the fellows and girls who make up the crew of *TekWar.* I've never enjoyed a filming experience more and I've never looked forward to seeing the finished product as much.

I dedicate this book to all my newfound friends at *TekWar.*

The *Tek* tsunami continues . . .

A ripple of enthusiasm from Marvel Comics' *TekWorld*, ending its first year.

A riptide of interest and the fifth book is in print.

A deluge of creativity and *TekWar*, the movies, are being readied for presentation at the beginning of 1994.

Causing all these undercurrents are . . .

First and foremost, Ron Goulart, who has aided and abetted me in all five books.

Fabian Nicieza at Marvel Comics and his brilliant team . . . and the wonderful group of filmmakers at MCA and Atlantic Films bringing to life on the screen fantasies that, until now, resided on the pages of the *Tek* novels.

And pooling everybody's talents is Carmen LaVia, agent extraordinaire, at the Fifi Oscard Agency.

Other invaluable surfers on our journey are Roger Cooper, Susan Allison, and Ivy Fischer Stone.

All of you have my gratitude.

One can only speculate on what the future holds . . .

IT WAS A rainy night in the late spring of the year 2121. As he flew his skycar southward, he said again, "I've got to find her."

Barry Zangerly sat crouched stiffly at the controls, both hands tightly clenched. He was a lean, dark man in his early thirties and he was heading for the Ocean Park Sector of Greater Los Angeles.

When the vidphone on the dashpanel buzzed, he flinched and jerked upright in the driveseat. Then, after taking a slow breath in and out, he touched the respond key.

An older, huskier version of himself appeared on the small rectangular picscreen. "So you're really going to this damn meeting?" asked Roger Zangerly. "You're a bigger idiot than—"

"Don't try to interfere," Barry warned his brother.

"You should let the cops search for Alicia Bower."

"Damn it, Rog, this is something I have to be involved in."

"Okay, allright." His brother was still at his office at the headquarters plant of Mechanix International in the Hawthorne Sector of Greater LA. Out the wide windows behind him you could see the rain hitting at the huge brightlit domes of the sprawling complex. "I didn't call to have a fight, Barry. It's only that I don't like to see you walking into trouble."

"I intend to find Alicia," he said. "She's been missing for three days. I just don't understand why her father or—"

"I work for Owen Bower," reminded Roger, "and, trust me, I know him a hell of a lot better than you do. He's very much concerned about her and even though he's in the hospital, he's—"

"Nobody from Mechanix is doing enough to locate her."

"We've got our own people hunting for her. And you know the cops are busting their butts on this, too." Lowering his voice, Roger leaned forward. "Don't get mad again, but there's something else I have to say to you. Alicia is, we all agree, a very attractive young woman. But, Barry, you have to admit she's none too stable. She was, afterall, in that institution last year."

"That was *last* year. I've been living with her for nearly ten months now and I know that she—"

"Actually this is my fault. Yeah, I went and introduced you two at that damn cocktail party. I've said to Dad more than once that I feel responsible for all this."

"Responsible for what, Rog? My being in love with your boss's daughter? Are you afraid that's going to screw up your—"

"I know quite a bit more about her than maybe you do," said Roger. "Before you there were other guys. A hell of a lot of other guys, in fact. She's never, you know, been able to settle down with one man. What's probably happened this time is that she got restless again."

"I don't want to hear any more of this crap from you."

"Listen to me." Roger shook his head. "I know you're eager to find her. But simply because you get a call from some anonymous hoodlum— Really, Barry, that's no reason to go flying off by yourself to a meeting in some damn slum."

"I'm sorry I confided in you at all. I had the notion that you were the sort of brother who—"

"I'm the best god damn brother you'll ever have." Roger's voice grew louder. "Maybe I'm not smart enough to teach at SoCal Tech the way you do, but I sure as hell know how the world works. Alicia Bower is just some crazy little bitch who's determined to sleep with as many guys as she can. You had your turn and she's probably just run off with the next one in line."

"Drop it, Rog."

His brother urged, "Forget about going to this meeting. Or at least wait until I can join you."

"I was instructed to show up alone. Don't try to screw this up."

"You never have, you know, been able to take proper care of yourself. I've always had to come along behind you and—"

"Go to hell, Rog." He hung up.

The vidphone buzzed again a moment later. Barry didn't answer.

He guided his skycar on through the heavy rain.

It was exactly 10 P.M. when Barry landed on the parking field near the Arcade. The rain was heavier now, slamming straight down through the night and hitting at him as he came hurrying out of his car.

Barry sprinted across the dimlit lot, which had only a dozen other vehicles scattered across it.

There was nobody visible through the windows of the ticket kiosk at the exit gate. Inside it, though, a dented and rusty robot sat on the floor. His left eye dangled on a few twists of red and yellow wire, hanging three inches below the rust-rimmed socket. Clutched in his left hand, which was missing a finger, was a sheaf of parking chits.

"Guess parking is free," Barry decided and hurried on.

A thin black girl, not more than fifteen, was leaning, arms folded, near the ground entrance of the Arcade.

Slowing, Barry scanned her. He was fairly certain that the person who'd vidphoned him this afternoon, keeping the screen blanked, had been a young girl.

When he was nearly to the entryway, the girl smiled. "$100 for an hour, $300 all night," she said in a gentle voice. "Blow job is extra."

"Thanks, no."

The first level of the structure housed fifteen or so establishments. There were cafes, betting parlors, saloons, and gaming rooms. More than half were shut down and dark. Less than fifty people, most of them young, were frequenting this level of the Arcade.

The plastitile floor was splotched with wide puddles of muddy water. As Barry crossed to the upramps, several drops of rain fell from above and hit him just over the ear.

The globes of floating light hanging over the entrance to the Level 3 ramp were smeared with dirt and one of them was flickering.

Far across the chill Arcade a young woman suddenly cried out in pain.

"Shut up, bitch," shouted a gruff voice.

Barry stepped onto the moving ramp. Roughly halfway to Level 2 it commenced making loud, ratcheting noises. Then the ramp ceased to function.

Barry climbed the rest of the way.

In the shadowy doorway to the defunct souvenir shop on Level 3 a young woman was huddled. She had her bare knees pressed tight together, her fisted hands crossed over her chest. There was a lopsided smile on her pale face and she was hooked up to the Tek Brainbox that was wedged in her lap.

"I love you, too," she was murmuring.

Barry had been instructed to meet his informant at a place called Gypsy's at 10:15. Gypsy's was midway along the righthand tier. Next to it was a small jewelry shop called Moonstone's. The shop was shut, its display window offering nothing but a long dead mouse.

The signscreen next to the door of Gypsy's announced: ALL THE LATEST FORTUNE-TELLING DEVICES & MORE! CLOSED FOR NOW.

Barry reached for the door. Before his fingertips touched it, the door whispered and swung slowly open inward.

In the middle of the dimly illuminated foyer, he saw the body of a woman stretched out facedown on the floor.

"Oh, god!"

He ran to the body, knelt beside it. The door shut behind him.

This wasn't Alicia. It wasn't a woman at all, only an android dressed in the costume of a gypsy fortune-teller.

When he rolled the android over on her back, Barry saw that someone had opened her chest and removed most of the inner workings.

At the back of the shadowy room another door opened.

Two men, large and thickset, came in. Then a big coppery robot, wearing a long black overcoat, followed. The three remained near the open doorway, side by side, watching him, saying nothing.

Barry rose to his feet. "Did one of you contact me?"

The larger of the two men nudged the robot.

Nodding, the robot came walking slowly over to Barry.

"That's why I'm here," Barry started to explain. "I got a call to meet—"

The robot hit him, hard in the midsection.

Gasping, doubling up, Barry stumbled backward.

The robot followed. Carefully, patiently, he punched Barry. Pounding him in the stomach, in the chest, in the ribs. Finally, when Barry had collapsed to his knees, the big robot went to work on his head and face with his metal fists.

Time got fouled up about then and Barry lost a few minutes. After awhile he found himself lying flat out on the floor, staring into the blank face of the dead android.

Someone was kicking him in the side.

Someone said, "Quit looking for her."

Barry lost some more time.

2

DAN CARDIGAN WATCHED the skycab climb back up into the rainy night. Smiling to himself, he ran across the apartment complex courtyard.

The uniformed doorbot who stood under the metal awning made a chuckling noise and opened the wide plastiglass door. "Second night in a row," he commented in his tinny voice. "And out until after 11 P.M. on a school night. Tsk tsk."

"You should oil yourself more often, Otto," suggested Dan, a lean, young man of fifteen. "It might fix that odd tsk noise you're always making."

The rain drummed on the awning over their heads.

The robot said, "She's an attractive young lady."

"That she is." Dan went on into the lobby.

He let himself into the apartment he shared with his father. "Dad?" he called, after glancing around the living room.

"Out here, Dan." Jake Cardigan was standing on the sheltered balcony, looking across the beach toward the dark, foamy ocean.

Dan went out and joined him. "You went there again today, huh?"

"Went where?" Jake continued to watch the black sea.

"C'mon, you know. I mean the cemetery where Beth Kittridge is buried."

His father turned to face him. Jake was nearly fifty, handsome in a weatherbeaten way. "I was there for awhile, yeah," he admitted.

"You haven't missed a day since . . . well, since two weeks ago."

"Since Beth's ashes were interred there." He moved back into the living room. "No, I guess I haven't. How was your date?"

Dan followed his father. "Don't you think you're maybe dwelling on all this too much?"

"Probably, sure." Jake sat in a low black chair. "Could be it's a sign that I'm turning into a sentimental old codger."

"Hell, you're not an—"

"Her death hit me hard. I keep figuring I'll get over it." He leaned back in the chair, then sat up again. "Afterall, Beth has been dead for over a month."

"You loved her and she—"

"I've got to accept the fact she's dead and gone, you're right." Standing, Jake wandered in the direction of the balcony and stood on the threshold, again staring out into the rainy night. "I've never been especially mystical or religious. But going out there . . . sitting in that chapel . . ." He shrugged and turned toward his son. "So how was the date?"

"Good."

"Just good?"

"Terrific then. You want me to review my date with Molly Fine as though it was a vidwall movie? Colossal, earthshaking, sensational—"

"You like her, don't you?"

"Quite a bit."

"She seems to like you."

"Fortunately for me."

Jake returned to the chair, sat again. "Spend as much time with her as you can," he advised. "And be sure you tell her how you feel. Because you never know when—"

"Dad, hey, you *are* starting to sound like an old coot."

"Overdoing it, am I?"

Nodding, his son told him, "You've never been the type of person to feel sorry for himself."

"Until lately?"

"Well, you have been moping around like a—"

"I'll reform," promised Jake, grinning briefly. "Where'd you and Molly go?"

"To a skyball game between our SoCal State Police Academy and Santa Monica Sector Hi."

"Who won?"

"Them."

Jake stood, stretched. "Now that you're safely back in the nest, I can turn in."

"Oh, I almost forgot," said his son. "We had a guest lecturer at the academy today. Somebody who used to know you."

"You didn't get into a squabble with this one?" Jake asked him, frowning. "Now and then you're going to run into someone who still believes I deserved that prison stretch up in the Freezer."

"No, this was somebody who likes you."

"Oh, so?"

"A lady named Bev Kendricks," answered Dan. "She told me, after class, that you and her used to be SoCal cops together."

"About ten years ago, yeah."

"She runs her own private investigation service now. It's nowhere near the size of the outfit that you and Gomez work for, but she has a very good reputation and supposedly does damn well. Very pretty lady, too."

Jake eyed his son a few seconds before asking, "You aren't trying to matchmake, are you?"

"Nope, Dad, no," Dan assured him, smiling. "Although she did give me the impression she wouldn't mind seeing you again. Maybe just to talk over old times."

Jake said, "You probably didn't get the right impression. As I recall, Beth was never especially fond of me back—"

"Her name is Bev," corrected Dan.

"What did I say?"

It was just shy of midnight when Sid Gomez got the call.

He had been sitting out over the Pacific Ocean in the glassbottomed cocktail area of Capt. Noah's seafood restaurant. The rain was hitting the clear domed ceiling; beneath his feet the dark ocean swirled.

Gomez, a curlyhaired and moustached man who was fast approaching forty, had both elbows on the plastiglass tabletop and both hands circling his glass of ale. *"No es verdad,"* he said to the blonde young woman across the table from him. "Which means in English, *chiquita,* it just ain't so."

"I speak Spanish, Gomez," Marny Selwin reminded him.

"I forgot," said the detective. "My point is that I've worked with Jake Cardigan ever since he came home from the Freezer and I haven't seen any sign of—"

"The fact that you aren't very perceptive doesn't invalidate my—"

"In the first place, Jake was never a serious Tek user. So there isn't much chance, even if your theory is true, that he—"

"Gomez, dear, I'm an Associate Professor of Biotechnology at SoCal Tech," Marny told him. "Most of the research in the report I'm trying to tell you about was done by me and my associates. Trust me, there's ample proof that Tek use, even on a modest scale sometimes, can cause brain damage. I'm willing to bet you that Cardigan's reflexes, his judgments and probably—"

"I can refute you there, *almita.* His judgment is obviously not impaired one whit—since he made the obviously brilliant decision to team up with me."

"I'm serious." Marny shook her head. "You really

ought to consider switching to a new partner. My study shows that people who've habitually hooked up to a Brainbox and used Tek chips to spin themselves assorted fantasies are prone to—"

"All I can say is that Jake is the best partner I've ever worked with," Gomez said. "As a cop back when, and now as a private investigator." Turning in his chair, he started glancing around the large, circular room.

"What?"

"I came to this bistro originally to attend the tenth wedding anniversary shindig of my cousin, Eddie Navarro," he said. "Then I ran into you, allowed myself to be distracted, became entangled in this deepdish conversation with—"

"Your cousin left a half hour ago, along with his wife and most of their other guests."

"I missed that."

"You were arguing intensely at the time."

"Wait now, *chiquita*. It isn't arguing when I'm simply stating absolute unvarnished truths. It's more a lecture."

"Honestly, I really do know more about Tek than . . . Now what?"

"I was trying to spot the bunch *you* came to dinner with."

"They departed right after your cousin."

"I didn't even get a slice of Eddie's cake."

"Were you hoping my friends would haul me off now? So you can weasel out of facing the fact that—"

"I never weasel." Lifting his glass, he took a sip of ale. "I'm more the fox type."

"I'll send you a copy of the report. What's your homefax number?"

He held up his left hand, shook it negatively. "We ought to change the topic," he suggested. "You and I haven't seen each other in nearly two long years, not since you did that consulting job for the Cosmos Detective Agency, and yet—"

"I actually like you, Gomez," she said. "I've never met Cardigan, but I've heard a good deal about the man. He may be a fine detective, but eventually the fact that he's addicted to Tek is going to affect his performance."

"He's not an addict. He doesn't even use the stuff anymore."

"How do you know?"

"He told me."

She smiled. "You trust the guy?"

"*Sí*, yes, I do."

"And to your knowledge he hasn't used Tek since he got out?"

Gomez studied the dark ocean underfoot. "Not much, no."

Marny laughed. "Not much? What the heck does that mean? You just now told me he quit."

"When Beth Kittridge was murdered by the Teklords—well, he did a little backsliding."

"The odds are he'll backslide again."

"I don't think so."

"You really should read my report, at least skim the thing. The statistical charts alone ought to convince—"

"Are you Mr. Gomez?" inquired the chromeplated

robot in a white sailorsuit who'd stopped beside their table.

"I am."

"There's a call for you, skipper."

Rising, Gomez said to the young woman, "Excuse me for a moment, *cara.*"

In the vidphone alcove he found a heavyset man of about thirty-five scowling at him from the phonescreen. "Do you remember me?"

"Is there a prize involved if I guess this correctly?"

"There's another annoying thing I remember about you, Gomez. You're too much of a wiseass."

Gomez inquired, "How'd you know I was here, Zangerly?"

"Your poor longsuffering wife told me when I called your home," answered Roger Zangerly. "She's not your first wife, is she?"

"Far from it."

"Right, I didn't imagine any one of them lasted long with you."

"Anything else that's none of your damn business that you'd like to chat about?"

"You handled a case for a friend of mine about a year ago," said Roger. "Harvey Conn, who's Junior CEO at Botoys, Ltd. We met at that time."

"*Sí*, I recall the encounter with fondness," said the detective. "You advised Conn to dump us and hire a competent agency."

"I was wrong. Turns out you did a damn fine job for Harvey—and you people were discreet about it."

"Ah, is one of your mistresses threatening to—"

"This is about my brother. Barry, my younger brother," said Roger. "He's—well, it's a complicated situation. They found him an hour ago in the Ocean Park Sector. Somebody's worked him over—more than one person probably. They beat the crap out of him. He'll be okay eventually, but right now he's in the hospital. I want someone besides the cops to work on this. A good reliable agency like Cosmos."

"Give me some more details."

"I'd rather you talk to my brother first, get his version of what's going on," said Roger. "Can you do that tomorrow?"

"Is he up to visitors?"

"No, but he can use the vidphone—so the hospital tells me."

Gomez nodded slowly. "I'll set it up with my boss, Walt Bascom, and we'll talk to Barry from the Cosmos offices tomorrow. Is eleven okay?"

"Should be."

"Until then."

"Gomez."

"Sí?"

"I know you'll do a damn good job," Roger told him. "But I still don't much like you."

Gomez smiled. "Wait till you meet my partner."

THERE WAS NO one else in the small chapel. Jake sat on a bench near the rear, hands folded and looking toward the rows of small copper-doored cubicles on the wall at his left.

The urn that held all that was left of Beth Kittridge rested behind one of those small metal doors. It was cubicle #27.

The simulated stained-glass windows rattled. A sharp wind was blowing through the morning cemetery outside. When the bell tower began chiming the hour of ten, Jake stood up, nodded in the direction of door #27 and started up the narrow aisle.

His son was probably right. Jake should quit coming out here to the Glendale Sector. For awhile he'd been able to pretend that this was a way to remain in touch with Beth. But it was growing increasingly difficult to feel that. She was dead and he had to accept the fact.

There was no place now he could go to be close to her.

He walked down the chapel steps into the grey, windy morning. The path back to the parking area led down across two grassy acres of cemetery that were thick with impressive monuments. There were angels, cherubs, obelisks rising up all around him. Each and every one no more than a holographic projection.

As he passed the knight in armor that was commemorating the memory of someone named Hurford E. Stone, he noticed it was flickering. The lifesize figure almost faded away, then snapped back into seeming solidity.

A gust of wind came rushing uphill, grabbing up several of the plastiblossoms from the base of the knight's pedestal.

A few hundred yards downhill from him a priest stood praying beside a grave that was watched over by a huge projection of a praying, widewinged angel. The priest wore a black robe and cowl and had on black gloves. He was fingering a dangling string of glittering metallic rosary beads.

Another strong gust of wind swept through the cemetery, catching at the skirt of the priest's robe and lifting it. Beneath the robe was a bright chromeplated leg.

Frowning, Jake slowed his pace. "Maybe that guy's just got a metal leg," he said to himself. "But maybe he's a robot pretending to be a priest."

Casually, Jake reached inside his jacket and rested his palm on the butt of his holstered stungun.

Just then all the monuments vanished. Someone had clicked off the projection system and Jake was now standing in the middle of an immense blank field of grass with the dubious priest.

Jake dived to the ground, stretching out flat.

As he settled into the wet grass, the robot yanked out a lazgun and fired.

The sizzling beam sliced a rut across a stretch of ground less than five feet from Jake's left side.

He rolled away from the smoking line that had been etched in the ground. Tugging his gun all the way out, he flipped over onto his chest. He aimed and fired at the robot.

Black robe flapping, the robot was zigzagging downhill. Jake's initial shot didn't connect.

Spinning, the robot swung his lazgun around to make another try for Jake.

Jake fired again. This time the stunbeam hit. The robot straightened up, right arm swinging wildly up and the lazgun firing up into the grey morning.

The wind flapped his skirt up again, revealing both silvery legs. Then, after swaying twice, the legs folded up and the mechanism fell over.

Jake remained crouched down. "There's still the gent who shut off the tombstones to worry about," he reminded himself.

Up above him an approaching skycar sounded. It was dropping down for a landing.

Rolling to his left, he looked up.

"Relax, *amigo*. Rescue is at hand." Gomez's voice came out of the speaker in the belly of the descending car.

It settled down on a patch of hallowed ground a few feet away.

Running over to the car, Jake hopped into the cabin. "Scoot over to the main chapel, Sid. That's where the controls for the monuments are and—"

"Too late, Jake. I noted two goons come rushing out of there and into a skycar as I was setting down," his partner told him. "No doubt they're the ones who shut down this conspicuous display of mourning. They're long gone in the direction of the placid Pacific."

Jake lowered himself into the passenger seat. "How'd you know I was here?"

"You're here about this time each and every morning," answered Gomez. "A fact that others besides myself are obviously aware of."

"Yeah, looks like."

"We've got a meeting with Bascom in a little over a half hour."

"New case?"

"*Sí*, and hopefully one that'll give you something else to think about."

"I wonder if that's why this happened," said Jake. "Did somebody want me to miss the meeting?"

Walt Bascom was a modest-sized man in his middle fifties. The suit he was wearing had, like almost all of his business wardrobe, a rumpled, slept-in look. He was perched on the edge of his cluttered desk at the center of his large, cluttered office in Tower 2 of the Cosmos Detective Agency. Out of the viewindows showed the other towers of this part of the Laguna Sector. Skycars, skycabs and airtrams whizzed by out in the grey morning.

Absently tapping his fingers on the saxophone that was sprawled across the scatters of memos, files and faxcopies collected on his desk, the agency chief said, "Before we have the interview with our client, gents, I want to pass on some useful background stuff."

Gomez was slouched low in a comfortable chair, feet up on a databox. "Stuff concerning Barry Zangerly?"

"Concerning what this case is all about," answered Bascom. "After you called last night, Sidney, I did some digging into—"

"You do have a home, don't you, chief?" inquired Gomez.

"A palatial one, as you well know."

"It's just that you're never there, even in the small wee hours. When I called late last night, you were still here."

"Actually, it's the only place I can practice my sax in peace."

Jake was straddling a straight metal chair, facing the agency head's desk. "So you already have an idea as to why Barry was beaten up?"

Grunting, Bascom stretched out his arm to punch a control pad on the far side of his desk. "Take a gander at Platform 3."

Over near where Gomez was slumped, one of the hologram platforms came to life. The image, full size, of a young woman appeared there. She was slim, auburnhaired and in her late twenties.

Jake asked, "That's Alicia Bower, isn't it?"

"None other," replied Bascom. "She's the only child of the widowed Owen L. Bower."

"Head man of Mechanix International." Easing to his feet, Gomez began, slowly, circling the image of Alicia Bower. "They're the largest producer of robots, androids and servomechs in the world. She must be a mighty wealthy *señorita.*"

"Four days ago she disappeared." Bascom touched a key and the image was gone. "Word hasn't as yet leaked out to the media. Her father is in the hospital and she was supposedly en route to pay him a daughterly visit the day she vanished. She never reached there."

"Kidnapping?" asked Jake.

"The police don't think so," said Bascom, shaking his head. "Nor do Bower's security people."

"Por que?" Gomez was sitting once more. "Kidnapping sounds like a pretty logical assumption."

"Not, they claim, in light of the lass's prior record," explained the agency head. "She's got a history of mental problems, for one thing, plus a tendency toward promiscuity." He shrugged with his left shoulder only. "The police theory is that she simply ran off with some lad and is shacked up at an as yet unknown locale. The folks at Mechanix International apparently agree."

Jake said, "But Barry doesn't agree."

"He's been living with Alicia for a year or so. His brother, Roger, and his pop, Bernard Zangerly, both hold down important jobs at Mechanix. It was Roger who introduced her to his sibling."

"Does her father approve?"

"Not so you'd notice, Jake."

"What about Barry's dad?"

"He's enthusiastic about the match. Probably because he's hoping his offspring'll marry the Mechanix heiress and make his position that much more secure."

Gomez said, "So you're implying, *jefe,* that what befell Barry is linked to the vanishing of Alicia."

Bascom spread his hands wide. "You lads will do the implying. I have merely been filling you in on some background facts in the case," he said. "It could turn out that he was roughed up by some disgruntled SoCal Tech students, who were unhappy about the grades he gave them."

His desk buzzed.

Leaning back, Bascom shifted a stack of infodiscs to get at a keypad beneath it. "Yep?"

"A Mr. Zangerly's out here to see you."

"I thought he was stretched out on a bed of pain over in the Burbank Sector."

"This is Mr. Roger Zangerly."

Bascom frowned, first at Jake and then at Gomez.

Jake shrugged.

Gomez raised his eyebrows.

Sighing, Bascom said, "Okay, send him on in."

"I decided I'd better sit in on this," announced Roger as he came striding into the office. "Hello, Gomez."

Pointing with a thumb, Gomez said, "This is my partner, Jake Cardigan."

Roger shook hands with Jake, brow wrinkling. "Have I heard of you?"

"Only you can answer that."

Bascom suggested, "Sit in that blue chair, Mr. Zangerly. Keep in mind, however, that if your brother doesn't want you sitting in, you'll have to scram."

"It's not a question of his wanting me," said Roger, settling into the chair. "It's a question of his *needing* me."

4

UP ON THE vidwall Barry Zangerly was saying, "God damn it, you have the completely wrong idea about her."

"No, it's you who has a totally naive notion about who and what this woman really is." Roger was on his feet, fists clenched at his sides, shouting at the image of his bedridden brother.

"Alicia is not sleeping with anybody else. She's in some kind of serious—"

"You're the only one who believes that. Because you're simply too damn stubborn to—"

"What you need is some air." Jake had come up beside the angry Roger. He took hold of his arm. "Right away."

Shaking free, he snarled at Jake. "Get your damn hands off me," he warned. "I intend to remain right here until this whole—"

"You can walk out," explained Jake amiably, "or I can carry you out over my shoulder."

"It's not very damn likely, friend, that I'll let you carry me out of here."

"You'll be unconscious by then."

"Are you threatening me?"

Jake grinned. "Matter of fact, I am." He nodded in the direction of the door. "You're disrupting the proceedings."

"But I have a perfect right to—"

"Mr. Zangerly," cut in Bascom, "it probably would be a nifty idea if you stepped outside for a spell."

Roger sucked in a deep breath, held it for several seconds before he exhaled. "All right, okay." Spinning on his heel, he went tromping out of the tower office.

"Thanks," said the bandaged Barry. "Roger and I don't agree on this, which you may've noticed."

Gomez asked him, "What do you think really happened to Alicia Bower?"

"I'm not sure, but it certainly isn't what Roger and her father's people think," he said. "Let me explain some of what's been going on. Alicia did suffer a breakdown of some kind about fifteen months ago. Rog is right about that, except—"

"What sort of breakdown?" asked Bascom.

"I don't have all the details. That happened before I really knew her—and Alicia's never wanted to talk about it that much." He shifted slightly in his wide hospital bed. "She was working at Mechanix then, in the Advertising Division. She had a collapse of some kind, and her father arranged to have her sent to the Mentor Foundation Psych Centre. That's back in the Kansas Region of Farmland."

"And *muy* expensive," observed Gomez.

"Did she collapse at the Mechanix headquarters?" asked Jake.

"No, at home."

"How long," inquired the agency head, "was she in Kansas?"

"Just five weeks. She came back cured, although one or two of her friends have told me that she seemed somewhat subdued to them after that." Barry shifted his position again. "Alicia and I have been living together for the past ten months. About two months ago she decided that she wanted to get into some sort of therapy situation."

"Why?" asked Jake.

"She was feeling depressed and, once in awhile, things that seemingly had nothing to do with her would upset Alicia deeply."

"Such as?"

"One night, for instance, we were watching the news," continued Barry. "There was a report about the accidental death of a South American politician. Alicia went pale, hugged herself, started shaking uncontrollably. That lasted for several minutes."

"She knew the guy?"

"No, she didn't. She'd never heard of him and couldn't explain why she'd become so upset."

Gomez asked, "Who was this unfortunate Latino?"

Barry thought for a few seconds, the fingers of his right hand rubbing at the bandages on his head. "His name was Antonio Corte, a member of the opposition party in Brazil," he said. "It was about that same time that Alicia started having quite a few bad dreams."

"What were the dreams about?"

"She could never remember them once she was awake," he replied. "Anyway, without consulting her father or anyone else, she started working with a therapy group down in the Venice Sector of Greater LA. It's a lowcost sort of operation she'd heard about, run by Dr. Harry Moreno."

"Did Moreno's group help her?"

Shaking his bandaged head, Barry answered, "Not at all, in my opinion. I think it made things worse, but Alicia kept insisting she—"

"Worse how?" asked Jake.

"The nightmares, for one thing, grew much more severe. She'd wake up once or twice a night. Sometimes she'd scream and then, starting about two weeks ago, she started crying out a name. Tin Lizzie."

Gomez narrowed his left eye. "Nickname for an automobile that flourished way back in the twentieth century."

Barry said, "She has no idea what the name means—whether it's a machine or a person or something else. But, being Alicia, she made up her mind she was going to find out."

"She hasn't, though?" asked Bascom.

"Not as far as I'm aware," Barry told him. "One reason I couldn't persuade her to quit Moreno and his

Oceanfront People's Clinic is because she felt she was getting closer to an answer."

Jake stood and started pacing amidst the assorted clutter on the office floor. "Have you talked to Dr. Moreno since she disappeared?"

"I've spoken to him, yes, and to dozens of others," he said forlornly. "I've also talked to the police and Mechanix security people and anybody else I thought might know something. I haven't learned much of anything, except that I seem to be the only one who suspects something serious has happened to her."

"Maybe because she found out who Tin Lizzie is?"

"It might be that, it might be something else," said Barry. "The point is, I know her better than anyone else does. Maybe she did see a lot of men once, but that is just not true any longer. I trust her and I'm certain she hasn't run off with someone."

Bascom said, "She was supposed to have been on her way to visit her dear old dad at the Salkin Private Hospital the day she disappeared. Did you see her before she left?"

"We were together that morning. It was a teaching day for me, though, and so I left hours before she did. If I hadn't, then maybe—"

"Did anyone see her leave your place?"

"Yes, about midday."

"She never made the hospital?"

"So they say."

"You don't believe them?"

"In a way I don't really believe anybody." He leaned back against his pillows. "They all seem to be talking about an Alicia that I don't know. She isn't like that at all. Not crazy and hardly likely to have run off with some guy."

Jake leaned against a desk. "But she does know other guys, doesn't she?"

"What do you mean, Cardigan? I just told you that she would never—"

"Does she have other male friends?"

"Yes, a few. None, though, that she's that close to. Don't you take my word that—"

"Have you talked to them?"

"Yes, sure, of course. No one knows anything."

"And there's nobody on the list who might've wanted to hurt her?"

"Kidnap her or kill her? No, none of them."

Gomez requested, "Can you, *por favor,* tells us a bit more about how come you walked into that stomping last night?"

"I received a call at my office at SoCal Tech," he said. "The screen remained blank, so I never saw who was calling. Sounded to me like a young woman, a teenage girl I'd bet. She told me she had information about Alicia Bower. No, actually she said Miss Bower. 'I know where Miss Bower is.' Then she instructed me to be at the Arcade in the Ocean Park Sector that night. Somebody would meet me at a place called Gypsy's on Level 3. I had to be there no later than 10:15, come alone and bring $2000 in cash."

"You brought the money?"

"Yes. And, no, they didn't rob me. When I woke up here in the hospital, I still had the cash."

Bascom asked, "Who else did you tell about the meet?"

"Nobody," Barry said. "Well, I told Roger. My brother and I don't get along all that well. But still, there are times when you feel like talking things over with your brother."

Nodding, Bascom said, "According to the police report, three gents worked you over."

"Two men and a robot. The bot did most of it."

"You didn't provide a very detailed description of any of them."

"Because I never got a good look at any of the bunch."

"If I sent somebody over there with a portable ID Simulator, could you come up with a picture of any of these goons?"

"The robot maybe, but not either of the men."

"Was it a Mechanix bot?" asked Gomez.

After frowning, Barry said, "I think so. Why?"

"Merely curious."

Barry sat up. "Can your agency get to work on this?"

"We've already started," Bascom assured him.

5

THE SLIM, BLACK woman came walking briskly across the mosaic tile floor. She halted, hands on hips, beside the table where Gomez was seated. "I hate Mexican food," she informed him.

The day had brightened and sunlight was showing at the windows of the Kaliente Kafe. Some of it was spilling in on the detective. "But you have a sincere, and justifiable, fondness for me, Sarge."

She sat suddenly down opposite him, warning in a whisper, "Don't use my rank, Sid."

"Sorry, Onita."

Onita Quillian took a careful look around the small, robot-staffed restaurant. "At least no cops ever dine in this hole."

"Actually the food isn't too terrible," he said. "Not authentic, but—"

"I'll just have a cup of nearcaf," she told the robot waiter, who'd come lumbering over.

"Sí, señorita," it rumbled before lurching off.

Onita rested her folded hands on the tabletop. "I shouldn't, if I wasn't loony, be here with you at all."

"Chiquita, we were once minions of the law together. Side by side we fought crime and chicanery in the canyons of—"

"Quit babbling, Sid, and let me pass on what I can about this Bower case," she interrupted. "Then I'll go sneaking back to my desk at the SoCal State Police office."

Gomez smiled broadly. "I was hoping we could turn this into a festive social occasion, but if you insist on making it all business—"

"You risk phoning me. You wheedle and cajole me for information on Alicia Bower. You practically sob into the vidphone. It's the first time, by the by, I've even heard from you in over a year. And now you want to pretend this is a date?"

"Forgive me. It was the sight of you after all these many months that made me giddy," he said. "I do, Onita, appreciate your help. Can you tell me what you folks are doing about the missing young lady?"

"We don't think she's missing."

"Eh? You know where she is then?"

The police sergeant answered, "Not exactly, but the theory is—and keep in mind that I'm not working directly on this one—the theory is that Alicia Bower has simply run off with one of her gentlemen friends."

"Nobody thinks she's been murdered or kidnapped?"

Onita shook her head. "The odds, judging from her record, are against her having been killed," she said. "And if it's been a kidnapping, there'd have been a ransom demand by now."

"Nobody's done that?"

"Nary a soul."

"What record are you alluding to?"

"Alicia's run off before, dropped from sight for a few days. Usually with fellows considerably older than she."

"When?"

"Mostly when she was in her teens."

"Hey, she's way up in her twenties now. Has she done it lately?"

"Not very often, but we—"

"Has anybody from Mechanix International talked to you about this?"

"Naturally. Her father is in a private hospital just now. But his security people have been in touch with our office here in the Long Beach Sector from the start. They've provided considerable background information."

"Info that Alicia is simply up to her old tricks?"

"They *know* her, Sid. Especially does Myra Ettinger know her."

"Who might she be?"

"The acting CEO of Mechanix. She's very close to old Bower and, according to her, practically a second mother to Alicia."

"Some mom."

"She's just being truthful," said Onita. "Your client is Barry Zangerly, right?"

"Your nearcaf, *señorita.*" With a lurch, the robot waiter placed a cup on the table.

"Thanks."

Gomez said, "We're working for Barry, *sí.*"

"He's a very emotional fellow. He's come barging into our offices more than once to yell at everybody."

"He maintains she's mended her ways."

"So she told him."

"Proof to the contrary?" inquired Gomez.

"No, we don't have concrete proof that she's been sleeping with all and sundry. But a lot of people who know her well say that it's likely."

"Hearsay."

Onita sighed. "You've met her, have you, at some point?"

"Nope, merely viewed a projection of her."

"She's young and pretty and you're smitten. You've vowed to protect her, rescue her, defend her reput——"

"What I want to protect her from is tangible threats. Like murderers, rapists and kidnappers," he told the police sergeant. "Sounds to me like you've allowed the Mechanix gang, especially this Ettinger *mujer,* to point you in the direction they want you to—"

"Look, do you want to come back to the office and talk directly to Lt. Verbeck? I'm simply passing on what I've been able to dig up."

"Your loyalty to me is admirable and won't go unrewarded," he assured her. "If not in this world then more than likely in the next. Did anybody spot her leaving her apartment on the day she disappeared?"

"Yes, a woman across the way and the robot gardener."

"How'd she intend to travel to the hospital to visit her ailing pop?"

"Zangerly says she usually took a skycab. As yet we haven't found any cabbie with a record of having picked her up."

"You don't think Alicia ever reached the place?"

"There's nothing to indicate that she did."

"What time did she depart from her digs?"

"About 12:40 P.M."

"No trace of her since?"

Onita hesitated, then answered, "No."

Gomez leaned foreward. *"Cara,* are you holding back some vital fact?"

"I'm not." She pushed back from the table. "I'd better be going."

"I appreciate your help," Gomez told her. "And your undying devotion."

"Don't be too sure about that last one."

Jake had remained at the detective agency. He was in Tower 1 now, holed up in one of the office cubicles of the Info Center.

"Darn," said the computer terminal that sat on the desk Jake was using.

"Something wrong, Rozko?"

Rozko-227N/FS answered, "I'm having a little trouble accessing the security system cameras at the Salkin Hospital. These not-exactly-legal jobs, you know, can be buggers sometimes. Meanwhile, while we're waiting, here's a shot of a couple of the Salkin nurses sunbathing up on the roof of the joint. Redhead's sort of cute, huh?"

On the three-foot-square screen appeared a long shot of two naked young women lying facedown on a floating sunmat.

"I'm not especially interested in—"

"You've been in mourning long enough, Jake, if you ask me."

"Rozko, there are several flaws in your character."

"Exactly. They were built in to humanize me. Do you want me to zoom in on the redhaired one?"

"No need."

Rozko blanked the screen, commenced whistling a Mexican folk tune that Gomez had recently taught him. "Bingo," he exclaimed after a moment.

"Meaning?"

"I've made it around the roadblocks. I'm scanning, even as we speak, the vidcam footage for the day in question."

"Getting anything?"

"It'll take a couple more minutes." The computer went back to whistling. "Gomez working with you on this one?"

"As usual, yeah."

"How come he isn't here?"

"Out in the field, checking with a SoCal police contact."

"That's right, you couldn't handle that. Lots of cops continue to believe that you sold out to the Teklords. Despite the fact that eventually you were completely cleared of all charges, they— Okay, Jake, I've gone through all the footage that pertains. There isn't a sign of Alicia Bower's having visited the hospital that day."

Jake leaned back in his chair, contemplating the grey ceiling. "Make me copies of all the vidfilm."

"You think it was diddled with?"

"I'd like to have somebody check," he answered. "While you're doing that, can we look in on Owen Bower?"

"You got it."

The screen went blank and remained that way.

Jake asked, "Don't they have a monitoring camera in his room?"

"They do, sure. Trouble is, it's blanked for some reason. Seems they don't want anybody getting a look at our tycoon."

Jake said, "There's something else I want."

"The redhead's home address?"

"I wish one and all would quit trying to match me up," he said. "What do you have on Antonio Corte, a Brazilian politician who died a couple months back?"

"Hang on."

A painting of a plump woman in a white gown appeared on the screen.

"What's this?"

"Just something for you to look at while I'm digging. I painted it myself. In the style of Renoir. Not bad, huh?"

"Lovely. Now can we—"

"Here we go." A photo of a thickset, darkhaired man replaced the plump woman's portrait. "Antonio Corte, age fifty-two at time of death. This is a publicity shot used by his campaign office. The next one's a trifle more grisly, Jake. This is after the fall."

"What'd Corte fall from?"

"The balcony of his suite on the fifteenth floor of the Hotel Maravilha down in Rio de Janeiro. He lived there."

"What did the police say about his fatal descent?"

"That it was purely accidental. *Senhor* Corte had been using a new medication to stimulate the action of his faulty plastic heart. The stuff made him woozy, say medical experts, and he took the long tumble. Thirteen stories to the nearest pedramp."

"What was his political persuasion?"

"Liberal. He was an opponent of General Silveira, who runs the country."

Placing both elbows on the desk top, Jake asked, "Any similar cases?"

"You don't want all the accidental falls?"

"Accidental deaths involving politicians or related types."

"Have you hit some kind of insight?"

"More like a very small hunch."

After nearly sixty seconds Rozko said, "Huh. That's funny."

"Share it."

"Turns out *Senhor* Corte was the fifth political figure to die in an accident in the past year." A succession of photos and copy blocks started to appear. "All of them liberals of one sort or another, all opponents of the Tek trade, all residing in Central or South America."

"They didn't all fall?"

"Nope, but each suffered an accident in the home or office, always while alone."

"Any link between the five?"

"Nothing that's showing, except that Tek opposition."

"Connections with Alicia Bower, her father or Mechanix International?"

Rozko answered, "Not a single one, Jake."

"Then why the hell did Corte's death upset her?" he wondered. "What would her reaction have been to the other deaths?"

"Tough one to answer."

Standing up, Jake moved away from the desk. "Print me up whatever you have on these five deceased gents," he instructed the computer. "Even though I still don't quite see how the hell any of this ties in with her disappearance."

6

UP ON THE roof of the landing area Jake was settling into the driveseat of an agency skycar when the vidphone on the dashpanel buzzed. "Yeah?" he said, tapping the answer key.

"Greetings, *amigo,*" said Gomez from the phonescreen. "Are you ready to divide up the chores of the day?"

"Was just on my way to the Kaliente Kafe to discuss agendas with you, Sid."

"Let me share what I've learned thus far, then you can do similarly," offered Gomez.

He filled his partner in on what he'd picked up from his police contact. Jake then told Gomez what he'd come up with in the agency Info Center.

Gomez said, "We have to talk to Dr. Moreno and Myra Ettinger, among others. Any preferences?"

Grinning, Jake said, "From the way you said her name, you're not too anxious about encountering the acting CEO."

"Executive ladies rarely charm me."

"Okay, I'll take her."

"Bueno, down to the Vencie Sector for me then. I'll be in touch with you."

Jake asked, "You think she's still alive?"

Gomez shrugged. "It's too soon to tell, *amigo."*

"She's about the same age Beth was."

Nodding, saying nothing, Gomez broke the connection.

The afternoon had grown grey again. Outside the vast reception room in the Executive Wing of the Mechanix International plant in the Hawthorne Sector of GLA, a dozen sooty gulls were circling in the overcast sky.

Jake sat in a hard metal and plastiglass chair. He was the only human in the large metal and plastiglass room. Arranged around the place were samples of twenty-five of the bestselling Mechanix products. There were robots, androids, servomechs. Nearest Jake's chair loomed a white-enameled nursebot. A small plaque pointed out that this model, MNSN/RT/39, had received seventeen awards of excellence from the medical profession and allied industries since it had been introduced by Mechanix International eleven years ago.

On a pedestal directly across from him stood the company's popular housekeeper android. Built to resemble a plump, matronly woman, HK/LN-232 had sold over

1,000,000 copies since Owen Bower had invented it five years ago.

After Jake had been sitting there among the mechanisms for roughly ten minutes, he rose up and stretched. He went wandering over to the viewindow to gaze out into the grey afternoon. There were only ten circling gulls now.

"Mr. Cardigan?"

He turned and found himself facing a very pretty blonde young woman. "Yeah," he admitted.

"We're sorry you've been kept waiting," she told him. "If you'll follow me, I'll escort you to Myra Ettinger's office."

"Thanks." He trailed her across the wide reception room and along a curving blank corridor.

"I'm an android," explained his escort, "in case you were wondering. You'll find me in the latest Mechanix International catalog under Receptionists/Companions. My name is Maxine/2140V/ELS. I was introduced only last year and have proven extremely popular."

"I don't doubt it."

"Here's Myra Ettinger's office," announced Maxine, halting before a wide neowood portal. "It's been very nice meeting you, Mr. Cardigan, and perhaps we'll get together again sometime. I retail for $146,000."

"Worth saving up for." The neowood door slid slowly aside and he went into the office beyond.

The room was nearly as large as the reception area and there was nothing in it except a single metal chair, a vidphone and a short, plump woman of forty-six. She had shortcropped silvery hair and deeply tanned, leathery skin. She was sitting, tan legs crossed, in the chair and smoking a cigarette.

"It's real tobacco, outlaw stuff," she explained as Jake was crossing the thick purple carpeting to her. "I buy them a carton at a time from a bootlegger down in the Borderland."

"I wanted to ask you some questions."

She exhaled smoke. "Do," she invited.

Jake squatted on the floor. "What do you think has happened to Alicia Bower?"

After a long drag on her illegal cigarette, Myra said, "Have you ever met dear little Alicia?"

"Nope."

"Seen pictures?"

"Yep."

"She looks very sweet and demure in most pictures. Cameras make her seem—what? Vulnerable."

"You don't like her."

"Not at all, not a bit," admitted Myra. "She's a spoiled little whore."

"Subjective judgment."

"I know, personally, Cardigan, seven men who still work for us who've slept with innocent little Alicia."

"Recently?"

"No." She exhaled smoke. "I have to admit that she either reformed after moving in with Roger's brother—or she learned to be a hell of a lot more discreet."

"Nobody hereabouts," said Jake, "seems to be worried about the possibility that she might be dead."

"She isn't dead."

"Any proof of that?"

"Only my gut judgment of her character. In the past, whenever the little darling showed up among the missing, she was always found safe in somebody's bed."

"Mechanix has several serious business rivals," he mentioned. "You're not afraid one of them has harmed her?"

When Myra laughed, she snorted out swirls of smoke. "We have a very good intelligence system here," she assured him. "We know just about everything our competitors are up to."

"Including kidnapping?"

"Yes, even that."

Jake said, "You steered the police to the theory that she has simply run off with—"

"No, you're mistaken. I only confirmed the dominant police theory. Lt. Verbeck's a longtime vet on the SoCal—"

"I know Verbeck. Yeah, he's been around awhile."

"The lieutenant has quite a fat file on her escapades. He's of the opinion that this is one more of the same."

"But he doesn't have any idea where she is this time around?"

"Not yet, although I'm certain he'll find her soon."

Jake got to his feet. "I'd like to talk with Owen Bower. Get his ideas on—"

"Impossible, Cardigan." She took another slow puff. "Owen is extremely ill, hospitalized. He can't even be bothered about major Mechanix business just now."

"Which is more important than his daughter."

"To us, I'm being honest here, it is, yes." She stood. "Let me add, in order to save us both time, that besides our own security people, we've hired a private investigation agency to look into this whole trouble over Alicia," Myra told him. "I agreed to see you today as a favor to Roger and Bernard Zangerly. But it would be against our best interests from hence onward to discuss any of this with anyone but a representative of the detective agency we've hired."

"Which agency is it?"

She laughed. "Being an excellent detective, you'll find that out soon enough, Cardigan."

Seven and a half minutes after Jake left her office, Myra's vidphone buzzed.

Picking the laptop phone off the purple carpeting, she touched the answer key. "Yes, what?"

"Has he talked to you?" asked the gaunt sixty-year-old man who showed on the small screen.

"If you mean the private eye, Bernard, yes."

"I think I better come in and talk to you about this."

"I've no time."

Bernard Zangerly said, "Damn it, Myra, this is imp——"

"Not as important as the other Mechanix business that has to be dealt with immediately."

"What did you tell Cardigan?"

"Precious little."

"Does he have any notion about—"

"Bernard, please. I really can't take any more time to—"

"Barry was nearly killed last night," his father reminded Myra. "That was not supposed to happen."

"We did agree, however, that the dear boy was to be discouraged from hunting for that little bitch," she said. "The fellows who were hired for the job were simply a shade too enthusiastic about their work."

"They could've killed my boy. As it is, Myra, they put him in the hospital."

"We don't want anyone finding Alicia for at least another three weeks, not anyone," she said evenly. "That's important to me, it's important to Mechanix. It should be important to you."

"Of course it is, Myra, or I'd never have consented to—"

"I really have to get back to work."

Bernard said, "I'm warning you that nothing more had better happen to Barry."

Myra took a slow drag on her tobacco cigarette and then laughed. "I'm amused at your selective concern for human life."

"You're, every damn one of you, to leave him alone from here on, Myra."

"He's safely on the sidelines now."

"But he hasn't given up, the beating didn't discourage him. Barry's still determined to find that girl."

Myra laughed again. "From now on we'll concentrate on discouraging Jake Cardigan and his friends."

A ROBOT TRIED to sell Gomez a souvenir.

The detective was strolling along the Oceanfront Esplanade in the Venice Sector when the rainbow-hued bot hopped into his path.

"Holoviews of the Venice Sec, chum?" he inquired, plastic eyes rolling enthusiastically in his metal head. The head had been painted a basic white, and then crimson asterisks, purple ampersands and golden exclamation points added. "Send 'em to your friends. Two bucks a pop."

"Do I, my good man, appear the sort who'd insult his cronies with views of this gaudy sprawl of mercantile real estate?"

Two android delivery boys came roaring by on jetskates, each balancing a large carton of Moonfood on an upheld, gloved hand.

The robot vendor said, "You appear, chum, to be a wiseass who probably doesn't have a single friend to his name."

"You've hit it exactly." Easing around him, Gomez continued on his way.

Out in the rutted street to his left a bearded air artist was creating an abstract picture of the afternoon with colored streamers of light, a lady magician was juggling a half dozen glittering silver balls and two deeply tanned men in their seventies were wrestling over the ownership of a plasliter of Sonoma Winepop.

Most of the buildings down here near the sea were constructed of realwood and true glass, materials that had long ago been salvaged and scrounged from other parts of the sector. On the slanting shingle roof of the Oceanfront People's Clinic three gulls were perched. Someone had dyed the one in the middle blue and gold.

In the reception room a motherly robot in a flowered apron was sitting in a rocker, knitting. "Things aren't as bad as they seem," she assured him as he entered.

"That's good to know. However, my purpose—"

"Even folks as obviously troubled as you, young fellow, can be helped."

"I'm not troubled," Gomez assured her. "Nor am I, alas, a young fellow."

"I'm Moms 1-A." She stood, placing her knitting on the crosshatched seat of her rocker. "There's no need to deny your troubles, dear. Why, I can tell just by looking you over that you're carrying around a load of problems and concerns. Those shadows under your lackluster eyes, for example, and those care wrinkles etched on your sallow forehead—"

"If there's one thing I am not, *mamacita,* it's sallow. Now then—"

"Moms, back off." A large, wide man with a full, grizzled beard had come shuffling into the small reception room by way of a side door. "Are you Gomez?"

"Sí, famous for my drooping morale."

"Well, young fellow, you look mighty hangdog to me."

"Moms was designed to be motherly, obviously," explained Dr. Moreno. "At times she overdoes it."

Moms 1-A returned to her knitting. "Don't mind me."

Moreno invited, "Come along to my office."

"Gracias."

"If you fellows want a cup of tea or some cookies, do give a yell, Doc."

Moreno led the detective along a narrow wooden hallway and into a small office that gave a view of the bleak afternoon beach.

Gomez dropped into the fat armchair the doctor had nodded at. "I appreciate your taking the time to talk to me."

"I'm very concerned about Alicia." The bearded therapist settled in behind his desk. "Your agency has a good reputation, and I'm hoping you can find her. That's why, frankly, I agreed to this get-together."

"Do you think she's still alive?"

After rubbing at his whiskered chin, Moreno said, "I hope she is."

"Any notion where she might be?"

"What have *you* found out thus far?"

"The law as well as the crowd at Mechanix appear to share the theory that she's done nothing more than skip off with some lusty gent."

"You don't accept that."

"If she's merely shacked up, why'd anybody bother to hire louts to beat up Barry Zangerly?" said Gomez, noticing a naked young woman outside, who went running along the beach and into the chill surf.

"I wasn't aware they had."

"Last night, concluded the exercise with a warning to cease hunting for her," said the detective. "This morning somebody attempted to kill my partner, which seems excessive if you merely want to keep us from finding the *señorita*'s lovenest."

Moreno rubbed again at his beard. "No, there's more to this than a furtive romance."

"Before we leave the topic of romance—do you know Barry?"

"I met him once." The doctor smiled. "A very intense guy. He wasn't all that charmed by the idea that Alicia was coming here."

"Would he harm her?"

"I doubt it. I don't think he's the sort who would murder her, hide the body and then come to your detective agency for help in finding her."

"How about other romantic figures in her life, past or present?"

"So far as I know, Barry's the only one in her life right now. As for the past—" He executed a massive shrug. "There's someone back there in Alicia's past that she's afraid of. But we haven't found out who that is."

"Could it be an old beau, an *hombre* who's come back to do her harm?"

"At one time she was fairly promiscuous," Moreno said. "There is, certainly, a possibility that one of the men she used to be intimate with has . . . but this is all speculation, Gomez. Nothing like that came out in any of our group sessions."

"What did come out? In particular—what about Tin Lizzie?"

The therapist shrugged once more. "As of now, only Alicia might know what Tin Lizzie means to her," he answered. "And she doesn't seem able to remember. It's somebody—something, perhaps—that she's afraid of, though."

"Did the name come up first in one of your sessions here or in her private nightmares?"

Moreno leaned back in his desk chair. "It took place here," he said, scratching at his beard. "Moms had popped into one of our group gatherings to pass around cookies. Alicia had been sitting with her eyes shut and, when she opened them, she saw Moms coming toward her. She sat up, put both hands up in front of her and cried out, 'Tin Lizzie! Stay away from me.' "

Gomez frowned. "But that wasn't the first time she's seen your robot, was it?"

"No, Moms is the one who had Alicia fill out the forms when she first came to us. And she's always underfoot."

"You've asked Alicia what Tin Lizzie means, of course?"

"Oh, yes, but she hasn't as yet come up with an answer."

"What's your opinion?"

"Only that it's connected with something important that she can't or won't remember."

The detective asked, "Did anything else come up in any of the sessions—even some small thing—that might give a hint as to what's become of her?"

"Tell you what, Gomez." He stood up. "I'll let you look at the three vidcaz recordings we have of sessions that Alicia attended. Because of our budget, I'm afraid we don't keep a visual record of all of them." He inched around his desk, moving to a small, jampacked bookcase. "I haven't had a chance to review any of this material since she disappeared, but you're welcome to." He picked up the three cassettes and handed them to Gomez. "I know I can trust you not to give away any of the other members' secrets."

"I won't give anything away, no."

Dr. Moreno shuffled to the door. "Come along, I'll install you in our viewroom and then get back to my work."

The room was small, wooden and poorly ventilated. Whistling quietly, Gomez popped the first of the trio of cassettes into the wallslot and then went back to his chair and sat.

On the three-foot screen in front of him appeared a longshot of the therapy session room.

Seated in individual chairs were Moreno, Alicia and three others. There was a lean, greyhaired man in his middle seventies, an extremely thin black young woman of about seventeen and a tanned blond man in his thirties.

Brow wrinkling, Gomez hunched in his rickety chair and leaned closer to the wallscreen.

"For the record, since we're cazing this," began Dr. Moreno, "let's intro ourselves. I'm Harry Moreno."

"Alicia Bower," she said, looking away from the vidcam. Her voice was soft, quiet.

"Ford Jaspers." That was the greyhaired man. He had the deep, trained voice of an actor.

"Everybody just calls me Slimjim," said the black girl, folding her arms.

"You don't have to call yourself that, Jimalla," the doctor told her.

She lifted her narrow shoulders. "It's okay, Doc."

The tan young man said, "Guy Woodruff." Smiling across at Slimjim, he added, "Hey, I like Jimalla better."

"I don't like Guy Woodruff as a name for this *hombre,"* said Gomez, his frown deepening. "He looks familiar—who the heck is he?"

Behind the frowning detective the floor creaked once.

He started to rise, to turn.

But the crackling beam of a stungun hit him high in the side. Gomez gasped, made a dry, gagging sound and then fell over.

8

JAKE WALKED CONFIDENTLY across the Service Landing field, which was at the rear of the multilevel metal and plastiglass Salkin Private Hospital.

Stationed on a stool near a door marked NUTRITIONAL SUPPLIES was a gunmetal robot. He wore a white smock, and built into the left hand that rested in his lap was a stungun. "Who're you?" he inquired of Jake. "Where do you think you're going?"

"Soyteen Food Products." Jake passed the guardbot a coded ID card.

"New?"

"To this marketing area, yeah."

The robot inserted the card into a slot in his metal forehead. His right eye flashed briefly green, the card slid out. "You'll find Mr. Maxwell Arnold on Level 2. He's the one handling the Soyteen account today."

"That's right next to the Control Center, isn't it?"

"Two doors down," answered the robot, returning the card Jake had paid one of his contacts $100 for a little less than an hour ago.

He entered the hospital where Alicia Bower's father was staying, walked along a blank, grey corridor to an upramp.

He got off at Level 2, went striding right on by the office of Maxwell Arnold, and entered the Control Center. The vast room was rich with rows of computer terminals, banks of monitor screens and at least a dozen servobots manning various control stations.

At a silvery metal desk near the doorway sat a human young woman. "Who're you?" she asked, eyeing him. "What do you want?"

Grinning amiably, Jake handed her a different ID card. This one had cost him $250. "I'm with Security Teletronics."

"What happened to Arnie?"

"Ailing. I'm filling in for him."

"Arnie's sick? What's wrong?"

Jake tapped his chest with his thumb. "Something internal."

"Poor guy." She pushed the card into a desktop slot. The desk produced a pleased *ping*. "What is it you came to do? Arnie just did the annual checkup last month."

Taking back the card, Jake explained, "A complaint came in to some of your people from Mechanix International. They're having trouble receiving the monitor pictures from Owen Bower's room."

The young woman furrowed her brow, wrinkled her nose. "That room's blanked."

"They just now told me from my office that the blackout order was rescinded," he said, sounding plausible. "Trouble is, the pictures still aren't coming through. Before I go up to the room, I thought I better check in with you."

"This is typical." She rose up, smoothing at her short crimson plastiskirt. "They never keep me up with what's going on. Let's take a look."

He followed her over to a bank of six-inch-square monitor screens. Each showed the interior of a different hospital room and a variety of patients. The screen with Bower's name displayed beneath it was dark.

The young woman touched a series of keys at the end of the row.

The blank screen came to life, glowing faintly green for a few seconds and then providing a shot of a room interior. The room, however, was completely empty, lacking even a bed.

"You sure," Jake asked her, "this is where they have Bower stuck?"

"Yes, I am." She walked over to a row of terminals, halting at the fifth in line. She bent, tapped out a sequence of numbers on the keypad. "Now we'll— Why the dickens don't they share any of this with me?"

"What is it?"

"Mr. Bower was signed out nearly two hours ago."

"That means he's better?"

"It doesn't say, merely that he's no longer a patient at Salkin."

"Odd that his own company doesn't know that," said Jake, feigning concern. "Where was Bower taken?"

"It doesn't say."

"That's the kind of jobs I've been handed lately. They provide me insufficient data." He gave a disgruntled shrug. "Well, thanks for your help."

"Tell Arnie to take care of himself."

"Very next time I see him," promised Jake.

He left the room, made his way back along the blank grey corridor. "It's going to be tougher than I thought," he said to himself, "to ask Bower about his daughter."

Gomez became aware, very gradually, of the scent of apple pie. He noticed, too, his skeleton. Every single bone in it, from the largest down to the smallest, ached and throbbed.

Eyes still shut tight, the detective attempted to speak. All that came across his stiff, dry lips was a groan.

"Don't go fretting yourself, young fellow," cautioned a maternal voice.

Reluctantly, Gomez allowed his eyes to open. He noticed flowers first. They were printed all over Moms' 1-A's apron.

Gomez realized he was lying on the wooden floor with his head in the robot's lap.

"How often do you have these spells?"

"This was no fit, *mamacita,*" he informed the robot in a voice that sounded rusty to him. "I was stungunned."

"Oh, goodness. Who would've done an awful thing like that?"

After running his tongue over his dry lips, he said, "I was hoping you could tell me. Didn't you see anyone pop in here?"

"My sakes, no."

"Then what made you look in?"

"That's simple enough, my goodness. I just now baked up an apple pie and I got to thinking, since you've been tucked away in here for over three solid hours that, why, you might be ready for a wedge."

"Caramba." He made an effort to sit up. "I've been out cold for three hours."

Moms helped him to his feet. "Take it real easy now, sonny. You still look mighty woozy to me."

"I am woozy," he confirmed. "That's one of the wellknown aftereffects of being shot down by a stun-gun."

"You're still sticking to that yarn, are you?"

"I was sitting here," said Gomez. "I'd just slipped the first vidcaz into—"

"What vidcaz is that, young fellow?"

Although it was painful to turn his head, Gomez managed it. He even accomplished a few stumbling steps. There was no sign of the three cassettes of Alicia's group therapy sessions.

"Okay, I know why I was knocked out," he said ruefully. "Next I have to find out who."

9

THE VIDPHONE BUZZED. Jake was about fifteen minutes from the agency towers, guiding his skycar through the deepening twilight. "Yeah?"

The phonescreen remained blank. "Jake Cardigan?"

"Right."

An image blossomed. A glistening, chromeplated robot in a white smock was smiling at him. "Are you available to take a call from Mr. Owen Bower?"

Jake grinned. "Definitely available, yep."

The robot smiled once more and then was gone from the screen. Next appeared a white-enameled nursebot.

"Mr. Bower has been extremely eager to contact you, sir," she said. "I'm glad we've been able to—"

"Enough bullshit, Bertha," cut in a gruff, raspy voice. "Roll the god damn phone over here so I can talk to him."

"You're not supposed to shout, Mr. Bower."

"I'm not shouting, Bertha. *When* I shout, the walls will rattle."

"Also, sir, my name is Babs/CGL-W75. Not Bertha."

"Babs is a candyass name. Who stuck that on you?"

"I've been led to believe, sir, that I was designed and christened by you."

"Hey, Cardigan, are you still there?" Alicia's father was propped up in bed, a large, big-boned man of sixty who'd lost a great deal of weight. His cheeks were hollow, his eyes sunken. "I look like shit, I know. Some kind of maverick virus—wouldn't be surprised if those sneaky bastards at Robotics, Inc. didn't cook up something and slip it to me somehow."

"Mr. Bower, you know very well that isn't—"

"Scram, Bertha."

"Where are you?" Jake asked him.

"I had myself moved to my beach house in the Palisades Sector." A wheeze sounded in his chest. "Couldn't tolerate those halfwits at Salkin."

"I'd like to talk to you—about your daughter."

"Why the hell do you think I've been trying to get hold of you for most of the afternoon?" he asked. "I want to see you, Cardigan. I'll tell you—most of the people involved in searching for her, and that includes the god damn cops, are idiots. They couldn't find their own backsides without outside help. Can you hop over here right now?"

"Sure."

"Give me the ID number of your skycar and I'll clear it with my security setup so you can land on the grounds. You know where this place is?"

"Most everybody does. The skycar number is HF/5532/HJM."

"I've got a hunch, Cardigan," said Bower, "that the two of us are going to succeed in finding my little girl."

"You're okay." Dr. Moreno moved away from the seated Gomez. "It would be a good idea, though, if you rested here for another hour or so."

"I've already lost three hours," he said, trying to find a comfortable sitting position.

"I didn't notice anyone sneak in to that room either," said the doctor. "I was in a therapy room with a patient for most of the time and maybe I missed seeing the intruder. Why do you think they wanted those cassettes?"

Gomez sat up straighter, remembering something. "That *hombre* in the cassette."

"Did you get to view one of the vidcazes?"

Holding his thumb and forefinger about two inches apart, he answered, "A *poco* portion of the first one only. However, the gent who calls himself Guy Woodruff caught my attention."

"That's not his true name?"

"His true name, far as I know, is Sheldon Gates," answered the detective. "I ran into him briefly on one of the first jobs I handled for Cosmos. He makes his living, usually, as a sort of freelance industrial spy."

Moreno scratched at his bearded chin. "Why would an industrial spy be hanging around my clinic?"

"Most likely he was keeping an eye on Alicia Bower. Mechanix International is a large, successful operation with a whole stewpot of rivals."

"You mean a rival of Alicia's father in the robotics business planted a spy here?"

Smiling, Gomez said, "That's only one of the possibilities. I can explore that and a multitude of others when I have a chat with Shel."

Moreno shook his head sadly. "He fooled me."

"Most spies are good at that. Got an address on him?"

After one more sad shake of his head, the therapist told him, "Woodruff/Gates lives less than a mile from here. It's a dilapidated houseboat docked at the old defunct yacht club. Hard to miss, since it's trimmed in neon."

Even though all his teeth still ached as an aftereffect of the stungunning, Gomez went ahead and ate the slice of apple pie that Moms 1-A had insisted on slipping him as he took his leave of the clinic. He hadn't eaten much at the Mexican cafe.

Most of the buildings he passed were starting to light up. The bistros, shops and art galleries, decorated with intricate twists of neon tubing and long tangles of lightstrips, were flashing multicolored messages into the oncoming darkness. At the corner a phosphorescent robot was doing a mime act, even though he hadn't as yet attracted an audience.

Gomez finished the pie just as he spotted the remains of the Venice Sector Community Yacht Club. A skinny man in the tattered uniform of a Brazil War soldier was squatting near the entryway out to the pier.

"How about some money?" he asked.

Gomez located a dollar chit in a pants pocket and dropped it into the man's hand. "Here you go, *amigo.*"

"God bless you, buddy."

"That may come in handy."

The houseboat was the only thing lit up along the swayback pier. Several other craft bobbed there, dark and silent. Sheldon Gates's place of residence was glowing, its outlines trimmed in long tubes of red, green and yellow neon. From inside the brightlit living room came the sound of music. A Mozart quartet, guessed Gomez.

He hurried up the gangway, which was trimmed in orange and green strips of light. The door to the living room was wide open.

Pausing on the illuminated welcome mat, he called out, "Is Mr. Woodruff at home?"

There was no response.

The music, it was definitely Mozart, continued.

"Guy Woodruff? We have an important message for you."

After another thirty seconds, Gomez entered. There was a lifesize holographic quartet at the far end of the room.

In the middle of the oval illuminated rug was sprawled the body of a man. A good part of the back of his skull was missing.

10

NIGHT HAD ARRIVED and the hillside Bower estate was surrounded by deepening darkness. Lights ringed the landing area, which was a white circle in an acre that blended transplanted and simulated jungle foliage.

Jake circled the area once, but received no challenge from the security system. Shrugging, he settled down to a landing.

The house consisted of a linking of fifteen plastiglass cubes of varying size. The walls had all been blanked and there wasn't any light showing.

Jake eased out of his skycar. A fog was drifting in from the sea and it swirled around him as he crossed the lot. The path through the brush and palm trees wasn't illuminated. The foggy night soon closed in around him.

A rustling started up ahead. Three figures, one carrying a lightrod, came pushing out of the dark jungle and onto the path. They were about a hundred feet from Jake, two husky men and a coppery robot in a dark overcoat.

Halting, Jake said, "Evening, fellas."

"Who the hell are you?" The man with the light played the beam across Jake.

"I've got an appointment with Owen Bower."

"The old bastard's in the hospital, hasn't been here for weeks."

"My mistake," said Jake. "I'll drop in again when he's feeling better."

The other man shouted, "We caught us a trespasser."

All three came charging at Jake.

The corpse wasn't Sheldon Gates, alias Guy Woodruff. Judging by what was left of his face, the dead man on the living room floor of the houseboat was Ford Jaspers.

Gomez had his stungun firmly gripped in his right hand and he'd already taken a thorough look around this room and then the rest of the floating residence before returning to scrutinize the body.

There was no one else aboard. In the bedroom there were signs that someone had hastily gathered up clothes, packed them and taken his leave.

The living room itself, except for the body, contained nothing unusual. It didn't appear as though there'd been any sort of struggle, and the weapon used to end the older man's life hadn't been left behind.

"But what's this elderly member of Alicia's therapy group doing here?" Gomez asked himself as he knelt beside him. "And here's another perplexing question—who killed him?"

Jaspers was still in possession of his wallet, which contained nothing but an ID packet, a Banx card and $90 in money chits. The only other thing in his pockets was a small tri-op photo of the Oceanfront People's Clinic group, complete with Moms. Gomez borrowed that.

A trumpet sounded suddenly behind him. Gomez jerked up and around, gunhand swinging upwards.

Louis Armstrong and his Hot Five had replaced the Mozart group.

He put his gun back in its holster. Halfway to the doorway he realized he was moving in time to the music.

Out on the deck he stood still for a moment and scanned the surrounding night. There seemed to be no one else in the vicinity.

"Perhaps the *hombre* I made a contribution to saw who paid a call here before I arrived."

He moved cautiously, but swiftly, down the gangway.

When he reached the gate, the ragged vet was gone.

The largest of the two men tackled Jake before he could yank out his stungun from his shoulder holster.

Jake fell backwards, sitting down hard on the path.

As the lout stretched to grab hold of him, Jake twisted to his left and avoided the clutching hands.

He then kicked out, his booted foot connecting with the lunging man's prominent jaw.

The thug said, "Unk." His head went jerking back, his eyelids fluttered, snapped shut.

For good measure, Jake booted him a second time.

Before the man was even stretched out flat on the shadowy path, Jake was on his feet and tugging at his holstered stungun.

But powerful metal arms grabbed him from behind, circling his torso and pinning his arms.

Chuckling, the second man stepped in close. Saying nothing, he slammed his fist into Jake's stomach.

Jake gagged, staggering in the metallic grip of the coppery bot.

"Pay attention," suggested the coppery robot.

The thug hit Jake again, even harder.

From the jungle to the right the beam of a stungun came crackling. It touched the thug's head and he made a strange choking sound, as though he'd been going to chuckle again and then changed his mind.

He swayed, fell to one knee. Sighing out breath, he went falling over sideways. He hit a holographic bush and dropped down through the foliage. He lay there unconscious with large green leaves seemingly growing out of him.

"Holy shit," commented the overcoated robot.

The beam of the unseen stungun found the robot next.

11

THE TEDDYBEAR GRABBED Gomez's trouser leg with a fuzzy paw. "Why don't ya buy me, ya simp?"

"Begone, *osito,*" he advised, detaching the toybot from his leg and replacing it on the low pedestal it had hopped off of at his advent.

"He's not for you," lisped the goldenhaired babydoll on the next display pedestal. "You want somebody like me, who's cute as a bug's rear."

"Actually, *chiquita,*" he said, squatting and holding out his palm to prevent the little blonde toyboat from leaping at him, "I dropped in here at Wondersmith's for the purpose of—"

"Gomez, honey!" A large, round woman with dazzling silver hair had stepped out of the back room of the toyshop. "Leave the guy alone, Lisa."

"I only just wanna hug him, Corky."

"Knock it off," advised Corky Keepnews.

"You're a brave woman," observed Gomez, "to put up with all this cuteness."

"It's nowhere near as bad as the bordello I used to manage over in the Pasadena Sector." Corky took hold of his arm. "C'mon into my office, honey."

"Want to play checkers?" invited a toybot clown as Gomez passed his pedestal.

"At some future date, perhaps."

"I'm on sale all this week."

As he settled into an armchair in the toyshop office, Gomez remarked, "These toys share some of the attributes of your former employees, Cork."

"Business is business, no matter what you're selling."

Wondersmith's was on the seventeenth level of the Westwood Sector supermall. The office's one narrow viewindow looked down on the brightlit University of SoCal Campus #26.

When Corky dropped into an armchair facing the detective, it made a surprised whooshing sound. "I've been doing some discreet electronic nosing around since you phoned, Gomez."

"You remain one of my best freelance sources of information."

She smiled broadly. "It was fees from clients like you, honey, that helped me set up my own toy business."

"So what about Sheldon Gates?"

"According to my sources, Sheldon's been doing a very lucrative job for Mechanix International."

"*Caramba.*" Gomez sat up. "That's a very interesting bit of news."

"One that's going to cost you 500 bucks."

"Give me some specifics as to what Shel was hired to do."

"I'm still gathering background on that," she said. "It has, though, something to do with old Bower himself and his screwball daughter."

"What about Harry Moreno?"

"Clean."

"No indication he and Shel are in cahoots?"

"None."

Nodding, Gomez asked her, "How about Ford Jaspers's murder?"

"I'm still working on that angle, honey. Nothing has come in yet," answered Corky. "He and Sheldon were in that loon group at Moreno's clinic, but that's the only thing so far that they seem to have in common."

Gomez rubbed at his moustache with his thumb knuckle. "As to Shel's current whereabouts?"

"Nothing on that, not yet. However, I can make a pretty good guess for you. And I'll toss that in for free."

"Go ahead, *cara.*"

"If Sheldon was involved in the knocking off of the Jaspers coot, he'll want to do some hiding out for awhile," she said. "Most folks don't know this, but his mom, who's a con artist of long standing, has been operating a beauty spa up in the New Hollywood satellite. She calls herself Madame Sonja at the moment."

"New Hollywood's that combo movie-making colony and tourist trap, isn't it?"

"The same. Madame Sonja's been bilking the rubes

up there for the past three months."

"Maybe," speculated Gomez, "I ought to call on the dear lady."

The slim blonde woman stepped onto the path from behind a transplanted palm tree. She was wearing a dark pullover and dark slax, carrying a stungun in her left hand. "Good thing I happened to be passing by, Jake." She smiled faintly.

"Evening, Bev." He rubbed at the spot on his arm where the toppled robot had been gripping him. "I didn't notice your tailing me."

"Because I'm good at it," replied Bev Kendricks as she approached.

"Picked me up at the Salkin Hospital, huh?"

"I was there and happened to notice you sneaking out," said the blonde private investigator. "I got curious and decided to follow you for awhile."

"So your agency is the one that's been hired by Bower and Mechanix to look for his daughter?"

"That's me." Kneeling beside the thug she'd stunned, she commenced frisking him. "Any notion who these boys are?"

"Hired goons. You don't know them?"

"Not even an ID packet on him." She stood up and back. "Seems likely, don't you think, that they're probably the same ones who roughed up your client last night? They're new to me, though, and I have no idea who hired them."

Jake jerked a thumb in the direction of the mansion. "Bower's not really up there, is he?"

"No, nobody's here. Bower was moved to his Bel Air mansion from Salkin this afternoon."

"Does that mean he's doing better?"

"I don't know what it means," she admitted, bending to search the other unconscious thug. "I only learned about the move when I dropped in at the hospital."

"Have you actually talked to Bower?"

"Only on the phone and briefly. I was supposed to meet with him face to face at the hospital today."

"No ID?" Jake nudged the man in the side with his foot.

"Not a thing on him either." Rising up, Bev brushed her hands together twice. "We better turn these hooligans over to the local police. And then . . ."

"Then what?"

"Does Cosmos object to your having conversations with rival agencies?"

"No, not at all. Especially if those agencies are run by former police coworkers of mine who are dear old friends."

"We were never close," said Bev, "but I *was* a friend of yours back then."

"So you didn't cheer when I got sent up to do time in the Freezer?"

Taking a step back, she looked him up and down. "You didn't used to indulge in self-pity."

"Let's go somewhere and have our talk," he suggested.

12

POP'S FLY/IN FOUNTAIN was perched atop a hill in the Beverly Glen Sector. The landing area covered nearly an acre, and the restaurant itself was a large plastiglass dome trimmed with neon tubing that sat at the center of the white-paved field. The silverplated, light-trimmed carhop robots moved from the building to the surrounding circles of cars on jetskates.

Jake and Bev were sitting in her car near the edge of the field.

Stirring her second cup of nearcaf, Bev said, "My agency is a whole lot smaller than Cosmos, but we're just as efficient. I'm going to win this one."

"Is that what you wanted to talk about? A contest between our detective agencies?"

"It *isn't* a contest, Jake, that's what I'm trying to get across to you." She sipped at her nearcaf. "I've got a substantial headstart on this Bower case. You and Gomez are never going to catch up."

Jake grinned. "I guess we better return Barry Zangerly's fee and head for the showers."

"Well, that isn't too bad an idea. I know you probably won't quit—but I still wanted to warn you not to be disappointed when I wrap this up before you guys can even get going."

"I'll alert Sid."

"How is he, by the way?"

"He was okay when I saw him this morning. After he hears you're going to trounce us, though, he may break down and sob."

"I like Gomez."

"Almost all women do, he has universal appeal." Jake tapped his forefinger against the side of his cup. "Where's Alicia Bower?"

Bev laughed. "That's one piece of information I'm not going to share."

"Do you know?"

"I have a pretty fair idea."

"You don't think she's dead?"

"No, not at all."

"Or that she's been abducted?"

"I've been on this a few days longer than you. I know a lot more about her background and character."

"Is Myra Ettinger your main source of facts?"

"She's one of them, obviously. Since, because of Bower's illness, she's the person who actually hired me."

"Is her version of Alicia's character backed up by what you've dug up so far?"

"Pretty much so, Jake." Bev drank some more of the nearcaf. "Alicia is a disturbed young woman. She has a long history of mental problems—and this wouldn't be the first time she's disappeared. Almost always with a man."

"Do you have proof that's what she's done this time?"

Bev looked out into the night. "That I can't discuss."

"Okay, let's say she simply decided to spend a few days with somebody. Why did that trio of goons rough up Barry?"

"To discourage him from looking for her, bothering her."

"And who hired them?"

"It could be the man she's with, who doesn't want his romantic idyll busted in on by a disgruntled suitor," suggested the private investigator. "Alicia herself might have sent them to keep Barry from annoying her."

Jake grinned again. "Has she hired thugs before?"

"Not exactly, though she is supposed to have a nasty side."

"After trying to scare Barry off—then she sent the same gang to work me over, huh? Not wanting me to interrupt her romance either."

"That sounds perfectly plausible to me, Jake."

"Has anyone threatened you or tried to hurt you?"

Her forehead wrinkled. "Not yet, but that doesn't mean—"

"You've been working on this a hell of a lot longer than we have, but nobody seems upset by your activities," he told her. "Even before I knew myself that I was going to work on this mess, somebody came after me."

"What are you talking about?"

He told her about the robot priest at the Glendale Sector cemetery. He concluded, "Tonight, to lure me into walking into this latest trap, they used either the real Bower or a simulacrum."

"Owen Bower would never be a party to any—"

"Okay, then it was an android dupe or a very convincing hologram," he said. "The point, Bev, is that none of this sounds to me like something a lovecrazed runaway is likely to do."

"Why not? Alicia has a great deal of money of her own, so financing it wouldn't be very difficult for her. And she's often run off with older men, *richer* older men."

"Do you have any evidence that she tapped her Banx accounts since she vanished?"

"That's something else I'm not sharing."

"Actually, you're not sharing much of anything," he said. "Frankly, Bev, I think you're being conned on this one."

"Why would my own client want to lead me astray?" she asked.

He said, "That's one of the things I'm going to find out."

Dan was in the living room with a laptop bookreader when Jake got home.

"No date tonight?" he asked his son.

"Homework. How about you?"

Grinning, Jake sat on the arm of the low sofa. "Mostly

business," he answered as he tugged off one of his boots. "Though I did run into Bev Kendricks."

Dan clicked off the reader. "I told you that you ought to look her up."

"She looked me up actually."

"Hey, that's even better. It shows that she's interested in—"

"It shows, Daniel, that she happens to be working on the same case that Sid and I are working on."

"You haven't told me about this new one yet."

After getting his other boot pulled off, Jake settled down on the sofa. He filled Dan in on the Alicia Bower disappearance and what had happened to him today.

When he finished, his son said, "You know, Molly knows somebody who's going to that Oceanfront People's Clinic. I bet we could—"

"Homework," cut in Jake. "You concentrate on that. You and Molly are, I admit, crackerjack investigators, but you're not to—"

"Dad, in one day . . ." He held up a forefinger. "In one single damn day they tried to kill you twice. I don't like the idea of some unknown hoods trying—"

"I'm not especially fond of the notion myself. But I don't want you getting tangled up in this," Jake warned. "And possibly that second attack was only going to be a beating and not a murder attempt."

"Oh, okay, great. Then I'll quit worrying about that one." He tossed the reader on the floor. "Have they identified those three?"

"Not yet, but we'll know by morning," answered his father. "They'll just turn out to be heavies for hire."

"I agree with you about Bev Kendricks's view of things. She's either letting them sidetrack her or . . . well, you know her better than I do. Could she be lying to you, trying to put you on the wrong trail?"

Standing, Jake walked barefoot over to the balcony window. "She was an honest cop," he said, looking out into the night. "That was some years ago."

"Then you suspect she—"

"It doesn't matter what she's up to, Dan. Gomez and I will keep working on this our way."

"Seems to me that you're dealing with a group here, some sort of organization." Getting up, he went over to stand near his father. "They can hire thugs, robots, androids. They knew you were going to be assigned to this case just about from the minute Barry Zangerly's brother talked to Gomez last night."

"Yep, I've thought about that."

Dan put his hand on his father's shoulder. "Are you going to the cemetery again tomorrow?"

"Not tomorrow."

It was long after midnight when Jake's bedside vidphone buzzed. He sat up, wide awake. "Yeah?"

The screen showed him a painting of a bowl of red flowers. "It's me, Jake—Rozko—coming to you direct from the Info Center at Cosmos," said the voice of the computer. "I hope I didn't wake you out of a sound sleep."

"Not a sound one, nope. What's happening?"

Rozko replied, "Oh, I had a little time on my hands and—yeah, yeah, I know Doc Olan is going over the security system tapes I swiped from the hospital—but I decided to take a more leisurely gander myself."

"Found out something, huh?"

A cartoon drawing of a smiling mouth flashed onto the phonescreen. "Not about whether the tapes have been futzed with," said the computer. "That's Olan's department. I did, however, notice something interesting. Give a looksee."

A shot of the main lobby of the Salkin Private Hospital appeared. More than twenty figures were moving about—visitors, doctors, nursebots.

"I'll freeze it," said Rozko, "and zero in on the galoot over by the upramp. I almost didn't notice him and then his red hair caught my eye."

The redhaired man was short, not more than five six, broad-shouldered and about forty. He was wearing a pale-blue medical jacket.

Jake sat up in bed and leaned closer to the screen. "That's Sam Trinity."

"Exactly what I exclaimed when first he came into my ken," said Rozko. "Next I asked myself why Sam Trinity would be playing doctor at 2 P.M. on the very afternoon Alicia Bower allegedly never arrived at this selfsame medical facility."

Frownlines deepened across Jake's forehead. "Sam used to be a field agent for the Office of Clandestine Operations, based back in DC," he said. "That was four years ago, before I went up to the Freezer."

"He's still with them. These days Sam is OCO's top West Coast troubleshooter. A very valuable gent in the view of many tricky Washington types."

"How the hell does he tie in?" Jake shook his head. "Is there much footage with Sam visible in it?"

"Just this one snippet. All in all, Sammy is only on screen for a tad less than three minutes, Jake."

"Unfreeze it, roll back to the first frame he's in and let me see it all."

"You got it."

The redheaded Sam Trinity came out of an office door marked HOSPITAL STAFF ONLY and into the large, oval lobby. He went walking briskly across the plastifloor and over to the upramp labeled Level 5. The ramp carried him up and out of the picture.

"Want to scan it again?"

"Nope," said Jake. "Level 5 is where they had Owen Bower. You sure there's nothing showing Sam up on that level?"

"*Nada,* as Gomez would say. I've finetoothed all the stuff I snatched from the hospital."

"What has the OCO got to do with this?" Jake rubbed his thumb slowly across his cheek. "Is there any way I can find out what Sam's current assignment is?"

"I've already tried that. The OCO's assignment roster has proved, thus far, impossible to access."

"Is he still here in Greater LA?"

Another smile flashed on the screen. "I had a bit more luck there," the computer informed him. "I was able to find out when Sam left our area—and where he went."

"So tell me."

"Samuel Trinity departed Greater LA the morning after Alicia Bower vanished," answered Rozko. "He flew out on a special US Military Forces skyvan. The van took off from a Maximum Security Section of the GLA Skyport."

"Bound for where?"

"His destination was Farmland, the Topeka Complex of Kansas."

Jake said slowly, "Which is where the Mentor Foundation Psych Centre happens to be located."

"Significant, do you think?"

"Significant enough to inspire me with the urge to travel," said Jake.

13

BASCOM WALKED DIRECTLY from his desk to the nearest projection platform. "Did you notice I've been tidying up my surroundings?"

"You cleared a narrow path amidst the clutter," observed Gomez, who was slouched in an armchair. "You're a long way from tidy, *jefe.*"

"But it is a positive step," added Jake.

"Took me darn near two hours." The chief of the detective agency turned on the holographic projector. "The identification of the goons who tried to stomp Jake came in about an hour ago, around 9 A.M." A large, widechested man appeared, life size. "You're seeing the ID footage of Leonard Rodney, last known address the Topanga Sector. He has a long, colorful record as a strong-arm man, sometime extortionist. He tells the law he has no idea at all who hired him to attack you, Jake.

It was all arranged by way of blanked vidphones."

Jake asked, "Does he admit also working over our client?"

"No, but Barry tentatively identified all three of these yahoos as the bunch that attacked him at the Arcade."

"Barry's identification won't hold up," said Gomez. "He's too fuzzy."

"I'm not fuzzy," reminded Jake. "We can still try to put them away for assaulting me."

"Next on stage we have Henry Weiner, age thirty-six, formerly of Berkeley in NorCal." An image of the other lout had replaced that of the first. "He, too, is a mercenary lunk and hasn't the faintest notion who hired him." Next the coppery robot, stripped of his overcoat, took his place on the platform. "This is Alex/762-AT. Manufactured by Mechanix International and sold, to the tune of 400,000 copies to date, for security and guard duty. Our particular Alex has been privately modified to convert him into a slugger. He belongs to Weiner, and somebody, Hank claims not to know who, erased all the robot's memories relating to any time prior to the evening Jake bumped into them."

Gomez inquired, "Did Weiner do the actual modifying and enhancing of the bot?"

"He claims he did."

"Then he's also capable of giving Alex amnesia." Gomez sank lower into his chair. "Of course, so is just about anyone employed by Mechanix."

"You trying to tie Bower's outfit into this?"

"They're already tied in," he said. "For one thing,

they hired Sheldon Gates to do some dirty work for them."

Jake requested, "Fill me in on this Gates."

His partner obliged. Finishing up with, "That's why I want to make a jaunt to the New Hollywood satellite."

"Do that, yes," agreed the chief. "But keep expenses down."

"I'll fast the whole time I'm up there."

Bascom walked directly back to his desk. He picked up a sheaf of pale-blue pages. "Doc Olan has turned in his report on the hospital security tapes."

"Were they fiddled with?" asked Jake.

Nodding, Bascom said, "Doc thinks so. It was an extremely slick job, but it's his opinion that about eleven minutes of footage has been snipped from various tapes. That stuff was then deftly replaced with simulated material."

"Of course, that still doesn't prove," said Jake, standing up, "that Alicia ever reached the hospital."

"No, only that some event occurred there that day that they want to cover up."

Walking over to the viewindow, Jake stood watching the morning city. "I found out that Sam Trinity was also there at the hospital that same day," he said, going on to tell them what he'd learned from Rozko.

"Sam is a ruthless *hombre,*" commented Gomez. "If they handed out an annual award for the nastiest government agent going, I'd bet on old Sam to take it in a landslide."

"He headed for Topeka Complex the next day," said

Jake. "When Alicia had her breakdown, that's where she was taken."

Picking up his saxophone, Bascom started absently fingering the keys. "Are you suggesting that the United States government itself sent an agent to grab this young woman and haul her back to the Mentor facility?"

"I'm only suggesting that something important is going on, something bigger than a girl wandering off." Jake turned to face his boss. "And I have a feeling I can learn more about it if I determine exactly what Sam Trinity is up to back there in Farmland."

Gomez said, "Jake's hunches are usually to be relied on."

Dropping his sax atop the clutter on his desk, Bascom moved over to the vidwall. "Okay, Jake, we'll book you on a flight out late this afternoon," he said. "Take a look at this now, fellows. A police connection of mine arranged for me to have a copy." He activated the vidcaz player.

Alicia Bower appeared on the screen. She was using her Banx card in a sidewalk kiosk. Glancing around somewhat nervously, the auburnhaired young woman thrust her card into the chest of the ball-headed robot teller.

The bot made a metallic clucking sound and handed her several fat packets of money chits.

Then the screen went blank.

"That was shot by the kiosk secam at 3 P.M. on the afternoon she vanished." Bascom turned his back to the wall.

Gomez asked him, "How much did the *señorita* withdraw?"

"$100,000."

"Caramba, that's not petty cash, even for an heiress." Gomez straightened up.

Jake said, "And this is supposed to bolster the theory that she's off with a boyfriend—that she was taking out a lot of money to finance a romantic vacation."

"It establishes that she was up and around *after* she was supposed to have visited the hospital," said the agency head. "And it does suggest that she may've taken off, wherever the hell she did go to, willingly."

"Is that Alicia, though?" said Jake.

Bascom blinked. "Eh?"

"Yesterday I had a conversation over the vidphone with Owen Bower," he reminded him. "Only it apparently wasn't Bower at all. Mechanix manufactures, among other things, androids. So—was that really Alicia we just saw?"

Bascom said, "Okay, I'll have Doc Olan go over this footage."

"I still," said Jake, "want to head for Kansas."

14

THE VIDPHONE BUZZED again. Myra Ettinger lit a fresh cigarette from the butt of the previous one, inhaled smoke, sighed it out.

She let the phone buzz twice more before bending to pick it up. "Allright, what?"

A small, slight man in his fifties, pale and wearing a grey suit he'd bought when he weighed considerably more, was glowering at her from the screen. "I don't understand, Myra, why you never answer promptly," he told the acting head of Mechanix International. "It's very near to being insulting."

"It might actually cross the line and *be* insulting, Jiri," she suggested, exhaling smoke.

"Must you continually puff on those things. Disgusting."

"Can you smell the smoke all the way back there in DC?"

Jiri Treska assumed a more rigid position at his wide metal desk. His office had no windows. "Do I have to keep reminding you that I hold a fairly high position in the Office of Clandestine Operations? You act as—"

"If you had a *truly* high position, dear, you'd be able to have a flunky do your phoning."

Treska clasped his hands tightly together. "I'm not going to allow you to distract me with insults this time."

"I'm, truly, not trying to."

"A lot of people back here—in the OCO and elsewhere, Myra—are very upset with the way things have been going," he informed her. "Keep in mind that there are still four names left on that list."

"I'm aware of how many names are left."

"Yet you've allowed not one but two damned detective agencies to become involved."

"One of those agencies," she reminded the government agent, "is employed by me. The dear lady who runs it hasn't an inkling of what's really going on."

"What about the other one, Myra? We've had run-ins with the Cosmos outfit before," the frail man told her. "Walt Bascom is a scoundrel, but unfortunately he's not our kind of scoundrel. The man can't be bribed or scared off."

"But his operatives can certainly be killed."

"Really now? From what I hear, you've failed twice to get rid of Jake Cardigan." He unlocked his hands and flexed his knobby fingers. "In fact, one of the ops working for you actually stepped in to save—"

"Jiri, my sweet, I'm awfully busy just now," she cut

in. "I'll make a note that you're pissed off and get back to—"

"This is more important than anything else you're working on."

"Oh, it is," she agreed, blowing out smoke. "But, really, Jiri, everything is going along smoothly and there isn't any need for you to keep calling me."

"If you damn people out there weren't so sentimental, none of this would be necessary."

Myra said evenly, "It's her father who's the sentimental one. And he, poor man, is not going to be with us much longer."

"I told him at the time, it would have been much simpler just to kill her."

"Despite having sold out to you people, Owen still loves little Alicia."

"If she had been properly taken care of back then—"

"She's being taken care of now," reminded Myra. "Please, let me handle this my way." She hung up and returned the phone to the floor.

Gomez stepped up into the Info Pavilion in the center of the main concourse of the Greater LA Spaceport. "I'm Gomez," he informed the pretty blonde female android behind the counter.

"And?"

He pointed at the nearest floating loudspeaker. "A voice from above indicated that a message awaited me here."

"Oh, you must be *Sid* Gomez."

"I am."

"Just hop into Alcove 3 on the other side of the pavilion, Mr. Gomez."

"Gracias." Shifting his grip on his single piece of luggage, a small battered tan suitcase, Gomez went over to the indicated alcove. After making certain that it didn't contain any sort of trap, snare or threat, he entered and activated the vidphone. "Sid Gomez here."

"One second, please."

"Hi, Sid." It was the hefty Corky Keepnews.

"What prompts this urgent communication, *chiquita?*"

"Can you spring for another 300 bucks, honey?"

"What kind of crass farewell message is this?"

The informant told him, "I got some stuff on the late Ford Jaspers."

"$200 tops."

"$250."

"Sold. Fill me in."

"The cops found the body this morning."

"Continue, *por favor.*"

"They don't know you visited the houseboat."

"What do they know?"

"They don't know who killed Jaspers," continued Corky, brushing at her silvery hair. "They don't know where Sheldon Gates, alias Guy Woodruff, is. They don't know yet that Woodruff and Gates are one and the same."

"Is any of this babble what I'm paying you the outrageous fee of $200 for, *cara?* My shuttle is about to depart and unless—"

"You're paying me the outrageous fee of $250," she corrected.

"Okay, but get to the nub."

"Turns out the cops have quite a bit of background material on Ford Jaspers," she informed him. "He used to be a vidactor, but he hasn't worked at that for over five years. He's been using a little dodge, which is what got the law interested in him in the first place—although so far they haven't been able to nail him. What Ford would do is join assorted therapy groups and play at being a very attentive and sympathetic listener. Then, after a few sessions, somebody was sure to blurt out some confidence they should've kept mum about. These nuggets of embarrassing info Ford then used to blackmail his erstwhile therapy buddies. It was a small-time dodge, but it kept the old boy going."

"Who'd have thought Ford would ever have sunk so low," said Gomez with a sigh. "Okay, he must have had something on Shel and tried to blackmail him."

"That's what the cops think. And it does sound likely, doesn't it?"

"It does, *sí.*"

"Okay, bon voyage. And don't forget it's $250 that you owe me, honey."

15

BEV KENDRICKS GLANCED around his living room. "This is smaller than your old place."

"I had a wife then."

She nodded at the suitcase near the door. "I hope I'm in time to save you from going off on a useless trip," she said. "That's why I stopped by."

"This spirit of co-operation between our detective agencies is heartwarming," said Jake.

She came up to him, tapped him on the chest with two of her fingers. "Damn it, this is between you and me," she told him, anger in her voice. "If my partners found out that I—"

"I realize, Bev, that I'm getting along in years." He took a step back from her. "But, honestly, I don't need any further help and guidance from you on this particular case."

Out of her jacket pocket she yanked a vidcaz. "I'm not supposed to show you this."

"Don't then."

Shaking her head impatiently, she said, "I want you to look at it." She extended the cassette toward him.

"Okay, all right." He accepted it, crossed to the vidwall and popped it into the slot.

Alicia Bower appeared on the wall. She was smiling, holding on to the arm of a black man roughly fifteen years older than she was.

Each of them was carrying a large suitcase and they were being transported upwards on a rampway.

"That's the Burbank Sector Skyport," said Bev.

"Recognized it."

The ramp carried the couple to an entry gate marked MEXFLITES. The screen blanked.

Bev said, "I'd heard a rumor about the existence of this yesterday. It comes from a random sweep by one of the port secams. I didn't get a copy until this morning."

"You've followed up on this?"

"Yes, and I'll be leaving for Mexico in an hour," she answered. "I know I can trust you not to try to beat me to her."

"I won't be going to Mexico," he promised. "But I would like a copy of this."

"Keep it, I made an extra. Show it to Bascom, but don't mention me."

Jake asked her, "You know who the guy is?"

"The name he used on the passenger list is Rob Stinson," she said. "There's a Rob Stinson who works for Mechanix at their Oxnard Sector facility. One of my operatives is checking on him."

"I appreciate your showing me this."

She held out her hand. "I told you that you were wasting your time, you and Gomez both," she said. "There's no need to keep wasting it."

"Nope." He shook hands, then escorted her to the door.

He popped the cassette, carried it over to his phone alcove. Calling the agency, he asked for Doc Olan.

Olan, a long, thin man with a minimum of hair, was wearing a white labcoat. "I was going to call you, Jake," he said. "About that bank-withdrawal footage of Alicia Bower."

"Was it Alicia?"

Olan gave a negative shake of his head. "I got some vid footage of the real Alicia out of our files," he explained. "From a society function she attended last year. Comparing the body movements of that Alicia with this one established—to my satisfaction anyway—that the lady seen in the Banx footage is not Alicia. In fact, Jake, she isn't a lady at all."

"Android sim, huh?"

"Exactly, yes. A hell of a sophisticated one, yet an andy all the same." A satisfied smile showed on Olan's long, lean face. "If you study the body movements carefully—well, nobody's yet come up with an android that can move *exactly* like a real human."

Nodding, Jake said, "I'm going to send you another bit of footage over the phone now. Can you do a rush job on it?"

"Is this yet another glimpse of the elusive Alicia?"

"Yep, in the company of an alleged gentleman friend. I want to know if this is a dupe or the real Alicia," he told the Cosmos expert. "And, if you're able, tell me whether or not the guy's mechanical."

"When you say rush, what—"

"An hour?"

"It won't be my usual thorough job, but I can get you a prelim report. Will you still be at—"

"I'm heading for the skyport," said Jake. "I'll contact you from there, Doc."

One booted foot resting on his suitcase, Jake was using a skyport vidphone. "Is there any way to find out?" he was asking Barry Zangerly.

Their client was sitting in a wicker chair beside his hospital bed today, looking somewhat better. "Alicia never mentioned anything like that," he said. "Why would they have built an android dupe of her?"

"Number of reasons—security, publicity," said Jake, "chicanery."

"You're implying that Mechanix is involved—her father, probably."

"Yeah, but it's possible Alicia never knew about the sim. Her father and other Mechanix execs sure must, though."

"This android—what makes you think one exists?"

"I've been through two separate bits of video footage of the thing," he answered. "Can you determine if—"

"What sort of footage do you mean? Are you sure it

wasn't actually Alicia herself you saw?"

"I'm sure."

"What's going on? You seem to be calling from a skyport. Do you know where she is, Cardigan?"

Jake suggested, "Let me ask the questions for a spell. Can you find out if Mechanix did build such a simulacrum? And if they did, what uses it's been put to of late?"

"I suppose Roger can help on that. Could you, though, please, tell me what exactly—"

"Not just yet." Jake hung up and grabbed his suitcase.

The Topeka Complex flight was boarding in seven minutes.

Roger Zangerly was sitting at his desk in his office at Mechanix International. "Yes, yes, trust me," he said to the vidphone. "I am calling you back on my tap-proof phone. Now suppose you tell me why I'm going through all this rigamarole?"

On the phonescreen Barry said, "I want to ask you something."

"If it's about your girlfriend, I have already told you every single damn thing that I—"

"Is there an android simulacrum of Alicia?"

His brother cocked his head to the left, then started laughing. "Don't tell me you suspect that you've been living with an andy all these months?"

"I'm serious, Rog. And, whatever you may think, I'm not loony."

"An android dupe?"

"That's right. Was one ever built at Mechanix?"

"Hell, I don't think so," said Roger. "Mechanix has, now and then, built special androids, sure. For, you know, celebrities, politicians and the like. As I recall, there's even one of Owen Bower that they used to send out to make speeches at sales meetings in the hinterlands. But it's been in mothballs for years."

"What about Alicia?"

"Tell me what exactly put this notion in your head?"

"Cardigan wanted to know if there is such a thing."

"Why? What the hell does he suspect?"

"He didn't tell me this, but I think—"

"You're awfully excited, even though you don't know for certain what the hell is supposed to be going on."

"I've done a little thinking since I talked to Cardigan," he said. "If they wanted to give the impression that Alicia has simply run off, they could use an android for that. It would be a damn good way to spread a false trail."

"Unlikely. Because why would anyone want to—"

"Listen, Rog, can you, as a favor, look into this? I'd ask Dad, but he's considerably more devoted to Mechanix. He'd figure this to be a betrayal of his loyalty to the firm."

"Whereas I, sneak and cheat that I am—"

"You're not as narrow as Dad can be at times."

Roger sat back. "Why, that's almost a compliment."

"This is important."

"Okay, you sound delirious to me," Roger told him. "But I'll do some sly snooping around for you."

"As fast as you can."

"As fast as I can without putting my backside on the line."

"I appreciate this, Rog."

"What are brothers for?"

16

REDHAIRED SAM TRINITY, clad only in his underwear, hefted the second metal case up onto the wide oval bed and smiled a thin smile. "You look bored, sweet. Are you bored? You sure look it."

The naked girl sitting on the opposite side of the wide oval bed shook her head.

"You can talk, can't you?" asked Trinity as he opened the second case with his chromeplated right hand. "Hell, I know you can talk. So when I ask you a question, I want you to respond. Are you bored? I wanted to know if you were bored, sweet."

"No, sir."

"No, sir, what?"

"I'm not bored."

He smiled again. "Don't you remember my name? I told you my name, sweet. Don't you remember it?"

"Sam," she answered very softly.

"Sam. That's right. My name is Sam." Reaching into the open case, he selected another artificial hand and held it up for her to see. "Do you like this one?"

"Yes, Sam."

"Give me an opinion."

"It's nice."

"It is nice," agreed the OCO agent, touching the hand with the forefinger of his real hand, stroking it briefly. "This particular prosthetic device is the one I attach when I'm doing an interrogation. Do you know what an interrogation is?"

The naked girl nodded. "Yes, Sam."

"Tell me then, sweet, make conversation. What is an interrogation?"

"When you ask somebody questions."

"That's right, good," he said. "This particular hand can administer fairly persuasive electric shocks. So that if I were to replace my present hand with this one and then touch you in certain places, you'd find it extremely painful. So painful, sweet, that you'd scream and cry and then you'd beg me to let you tell me every single damn thing you knew. Would you like me to give you a demonstration of how it works?"

"No, Sam."

"No?" He carefully arranged the hand on the bed, in line with the eight other electronic hands that were already on display there. "What sort of whore are you? They told me you were the sort of whore who'd do anything. Isn't that true, sweet? If I wanted to caress you with this particular hand of mine, wouldn't you go along? Would you make me call up your pimp and ask for my money back?"

"I'd go along, Sam."

"That's better." He reached into the second case for another of his hands to show her. "Actually, sweet, all I want to do right now is give you a look. You are enjoying this display, aren't you?"

"Yes, Sam."

"Yes, Sam, what?"

"Yes, Sam, I'm enjoying it."

"Very much?"

"Yes, very much."

"Good, because it isn't enough that I have a good time with the whore I hire for the night. No, I want my whore for the night to have a good time, too."

"I am."

"You're what?"

"I'm having a good time."

"Why are you shivering then?"

"Well, it's a little chilly here in your bedroom."

"Is it? I happen to like it this way. Don't you?"

"Yes, Sam."

"Now this hand here has a lazgun built in," he explained, holding it up. "It looks, however, like just a regular everyday hand. It resembles, in fact, the hand I lost in the line of duty seven years ago. But there's a lazgun built into this finger. I can use this hand to kill anyone I want. It always surprises them, they never expect it. Because it looks so much like a real hand. It would surprise you, wouldn't it?"

"No, Sam."

"It wouldn't surprise you, sweet? Why wouldn't it surprise you?"

"Because you just showed it to me and I'd be expecting it," the naked girl answered.

"You're absolutely right. I did spoil the surprise by—"

The vidphone over in the alcove buzzed.

"That's my emergency line," said Trinity, placing the hand on the bed. "Will you excuse me?"

"Yes, I'll excuse you."

"That's very thoughtful and I appreciate it." He hurried barefooted over to the phone. "Yes?"

"Lord, Sam, put something on," suggested Myra Ettinger. "Seeing that wealth of red fuzz that covers your squatty body makes one—"

"You're no pastoral sunset yourself, sweet, even when fully clothed. Why are you bothering me?"

"I have something to tell you."

The redheaded government agent said, "You happen to be intruding on my recreation time."

"Nevertheless, pay attention," said the Mechanix executive. "Jake Cardigan left Greater Los Angeles an hour ago and, according to my sources, he's headed for Topeka Complex."

"Coming here, huh?" Trinity made a faint whistling sound. "That son of a bitch is smarter than I thought."

"Or you're dumber."

Trinity said, "Thanks for alerting me, sweet."

"It might be a good idea to meet him when he lands and—"

"Naw, I don't operate that obviously. You should know by now that I'm inclined toward subtlety."

"Seeing you standing there in your undies misled me."

Trinity smiled. "Cardigan will be checking in with contacts in Farmland. He'll be checking in with people who can provide information and assistance. What I have to do is arrange some surprises for Cardigan, possibly making use of one of his cronies or informants."

"Why not simply grab him and—"

"Good bye, Myra." The agent hung up and walked, slowly, back toward the bed. "Go home, sweet."

"Okay, Sam."

"This ought to make you sad. Does it make you sad that you won't be spending the night with me?"

"Yes, Sam," answered the naked girl, getting up from the bed, "it makes me sad."

Shifting in the chair in the vidphone alcove of his hotel suite, Jake made another call on the tap-proof phone. It was a little after 11 P.M. and he'd been in Topeka Complex for over an hour. This was his fifth call.

"Hello?" The screen remained blank.

"I'm trying to reach Joe Chatman."

"Jake! What the hell are you doing in Farmland?" A heavyset black man showed on the screen. He didn't have any legs and was seated in a chromeplated wheelchair.

Jake let out a breath. "Joe, I hadn't heard that—"

"Happened while you were away."

"How?"

"I still, you know, got my vidwall show on the Underground Network," Chatman said. "Year ago—thirteen months actually—I was doing another of my muckraking series. This one was about some possible links between local Tek cartels and our major business giant in these parts, the revered Farmboy Industries. The bastards used one of those kamikaze androids on me, a simulacrum of my sister. I was really stupid and— Oh, shit, Jake, I'm sorry."

"That's okay." He turned away from the screen for a few seconds. "In a way, Beth was stupid, too. To have fallen in love with me in the first place and then to have accepted that android dupe of me as—"

"No, I don't think she was," said Chatman. "They can really catch you off guard. My sister, you know, had been real sick and when I saw her coming toward me in that supermall and looking so poorly, you know, I rushed up and put my arms around her."

"You survived, though."

"Part of me survived anyway. That was only because that particular kamikaze didn't work quite right and only part of the explosive charge went off."

"I was going to ask for some help on a case, but maybe you—"

"There's still enough of me left to do you some favors," Chatman assured him. "You helped me lots of times back when I was doing my show out in Greater LA. I hear you're working for Bascom at Cosmos now. Is this a job for them?"

"Yeah, we've been hired to find Alicia Bower. She's the Mechanix heiress and has been missing for—"

"I already heard a rumor about that," cut in his friend. "You think she's around here someplace?"

"Supposedly she had a breakdown a year or so back. She did some time in the Mentor Psych Centre," said Jake. "I don't know if she was taken there again, but I do know that Sam Trinity of the OCO was in Greater Los Angeles the day she disappeared and at the same place she was supposed to be. It's possible, for some reason I don't yet know, that he brought her here."

"Trinity is a true-blue bastard," warned Chatman. "If you're planning to go up against him, you know, you'll have to be damn careful."

"Right now, Joe, I'm looking for a way to find out what's going on inside the Centre."

Leaning back, Chatman closed his eyes for several seconds, fingertips drumming on the arms of his wheelchair. "I been thinking about doing a series on that place."

"Is something wrong going on there?"

"That could be, you know," answered Chatman. "I do have a contact. Maybe, I'm not absolutely sure, you know, but possibly I can arrange for you two to get together. That might help you find out some of what you want—with some scuttlebutt left over for me to use on a broadcast."

"Can you set up a meeting?"

"This person has to be, you know, extremely careful," his friend said. "Still, Jake, I can probably arrange something for tomorrow. You stand by and I'll get back in touch."

Jake grinned. "I appreciate this."

"I'll be talking to you tomorrow then. And, you know, I surely didn't mean to imply that your ladyfriend was—"

"I know. Good night, Joe."

Jake made three more calls before turning in.

17

THE PHONE AWAKENED Jake at a few minutes before 6 A.M. He rolled out of his bed, grabbed up his trousers and hurried over to answer it. "Yeah?"

"Is Jake Cardigan there?" inquired the blonde, freckled woman on the phonescreen.

"I'm Cardigan."

"Unblank, so I can get a look at you."

"Soon as I get my pants on."

"I was told your phone is tap-proof."

"Yep, it is."

"So is mine. I'm Dr. Sharon Harker," she told him. "Are you interested in information about the Mentor setup?"

He had his pants tugged all the way on. He touched the key that allowed her to see him. "I am, yes."

"You look pretty much like the pictures I was shown,"

decided Dr. Harker after a few seconds. “Older, of course.”

He grinned. “When you get through reflecting on the ravages of time,” he suggested, “tell me who’s been talking to you about me.”

She shook her head. “Somebody who . . . No, Sean, Mama’s on the phone now. Play with your skycar.”

A yellowhaired boy of about three showed up beside her. He was clad in crimson pajamas, carrying a toy skycar and frowning deeply. “Want breakfast,” he told his mother.

“In just a very few minutes, dear,” she promised. “As soon as I finish my call.”

“Is that Beepaw?” he asked, staring directly at Jake.

“No, it’s only a friend of mine.”

“Can I talk to Beepaw?”

“We’ll call Grandpa later. You go play in your room.”

“Bye, Beepaw.” The little boy wandered out of range.

“Excuse me,” she said, smiling at Jake. “Listen, I have some information that’ll be helpful to you.”

“You selling?”

“No.” An angry expression touched her freckled face. “No, I’m simply interested in seeing that—well, I’m sorry if this sounds youthful and naive. I believe, though, that something wrong is going on there and that action should be taken. Maybe you’re the one who can fix things.”

“Do you work at Mentor?”

“Don’t pick that up, Sean,” she called. “No, I’m an executive with Sunnyland Medical Equipment. I make frequent visits to Mentor, however, in the line of work.

Could you possibly meet me this morning? I'd like to talk to you where nobody can interrupt or disturb us."

"This has to do with Alicia Bower?"

"Yes, obviously, or otherwise, Mr. Cardigan, I wouldn't be bothering you," said Dr. Harker. "Do you know where the Prairie is?"

"That's Farmboy Industries' biggest facility in these parts, isn't it?"

"Right, two hundred acres of buildings devoted to the manufacture of synthetic food." Her nose wrinkled. "I have to do business with them, too, and I'll be calling there this morning. A block south of the Prairie you'll find a nice little place called the Grange Cafe. If you can meet me there in an hour, I can tell you things that should help you with the case you're working on."

"Is Alicia at Mentor?"

"One hour." The screen went blank.

"Okay, one hour." Jake put on the rest of his clothes.

The Grange Cafe was wedged midblock in a row of narrow shops. The chill, grey block was empty of people as Jake approached the meeting place on foot.

He found the plastiglass front wall of the little restaurant blanked. A signscreen on the door told him: TEMPORARILY CLOSED. WILL REOPEN SOON.

Frowning, Jake glanced around the early morning street. Sharon Harker was nowhere in sight.

From where he stood he could see the tops of the Prairie's towers and domes. This agricultural complex turned out nearly half of Farmboy's synthetic wheat and oats. Thin wisps of pale blue smoke were snaking up from its many filtered smokestacks.

Jake, thrusting his fists into his jacket pockets, walked toward the nearest corner. All the shops had blanked walls and many of them displayed signs announcing they weren't opening today.

"You there, sir."

Coming at him from around the corner was a large gunmetal robot with *Street Patrol* lettered large across the front of him.

"Yeah?"

"ID packet, please."

"Why?"

"Routine, sir."

"You'll need a better reason than that."

The big bot said, "We'd like to know what you're doing in this area."

Nodding back in the direction of the restaurant, he said, "I was planning to have breakfast at the Grange, but it appears to be shut tight. Can you suggest another spot where—"

"The best thing for you to do, sir, is hightail it clean out of this . . . Hold on. Looks like it's too late."

A distant rumbling had become audible. It sounded as though quite a few heavy vehicles were roaring this way.

Over at the Prairie, huge panels began sliding open in the nearest domes. Rising up out of the complex came silvery skyvans, each with the familiar Farmboy logo—a farmer's strawhat with a crossed knife and fork beneath it—emblazoned on its underside. By the time a full two dozen of the flying vans had taken to the air, heavy landtrucks were growling into view along the street.

There were at least ten of the big trucks, and marching alongside, between and in front of them were hundreds of men and women. All of them were clad in tan coveralls. Considerable flashing lightsigns were to be seen, held aloft by the marchers—*Farmboy UNFAIR! Work HAZARDS Must Stop! A Harvest of Shame!*

"It's the strike, sir," warned the robot. "You'd better get on out of their way before—"

"C'mon, join us." A large black man grabbed Jake by the arm as he came tramping by.

"It's no doubt a good cause," said Jake as he was dragged into and became part of the marching crowd. "But it's not my cause."

"Here, carry this." A heavyset blonde woman thrust the staff of a lightsign into his hands.

The sign was blinking the message—*INHUMAN Working Conditions! We're NOT Bots!*

The skyvans from the Prairie were hovering overhead. From loudspeakers mounted near the logo came a booming metallic voice. It echoed and bounced all around the strikers. "This is a wildcat strike. The Board of Directors of your Farmhands Union, Local #1343, does not sanction your actions. Disperse at once or face the consequences."

"We're coming in!" shouted the marching strikers.

"Discontinue and scatter. At once."

Thirty seconds later the barrels of stuncannons started protruding from the bellies of the hovering vans. The guns fired down randomly. A lean, bearded man in front of Jake was struck by one of the sizzling beams. He took two jerking steps ahead, clenched his fists, went slamming down on his knees. He started to topple to the left, right into the path of a rolling truck.

Dropping his sign, Jake leaped and caught the man by the collar of his coveralls. He yanked him clear of of the big truck.

Hefting the unconscious worker over his shoulder, Jake started to push his way through the moving crowd. "Hey, let me get him over to the sidewalk."

Another random beam struck a girl a few feet from Jake. Gagging, she tried to reach for her throat. Then she collapsed, falling right into Jake.

There was no room to dodge and he tripped over her. He fell, dropping the man he was trying to carry to safety.

He landed on elbows and knees, smacking the street hard. Someone stepped on his back, someone else kicked his shoulder.

Jake, a little groggy, was pushing himself up when someone yelled, "Gas!"

Jake never saw the stuff, but for about the next thirty seconds he was aware of a harsh, insinuating peppery scent.

Then he went suddenly and completely to sleep.

18

IT WAS ALWAYS sunny noontime on New Hollywood. The streets on the orbiting satellite were wide and lined with tall, simulated palm trees, the buildings were mostly white with bright red tile roofs. There seemed to be low green hills beyond the city, and off to the west was a glimpse of placid blue ocean.

The robot driver of the landbus was wearing a yellow and green checkered sportcoat. "And on our left, ladies and gentlemen, is the Holographic Hollywood Star Museum, containing lifelike images of over one hundred movie and vidwall stars from the past three centuries."

"We have to see that, too, Inez," said the excited fat man seated just behind Gomez.

"I was afraid we would, Lloyd."

The robot driver continued, "Coming up on our

right, ladies and gentlemen, you'll note the Stunt Palace with its FX Annex. Every hour of the day you can witness and enjoy pulsepounding, nervewracking stunts and special effects being re-created before your very eyes."

"Not before *my* eyes," stated Inez.

"C'mon, we came here to enjoy it *all,*" pleaded Lloyd.

"Next, ladies and gentlemen, is the Cowboy Heaven Museum. Then, for the more mature visitor to New Hollywood, you'll find Sunset Strippers. It is, as most of you no doubt know, one of the most popular brothels on or off the Earth. Here you'll encounter for your pleasure android replicas of all your favorite actors and actresses of today and, for a surprisingly nominal fee, you may do with them as you will."

"We'll skip that one, Lloyd."

The bus halted in front of a five-story stucco and red tile structure. "Here's the New Hollywood Hotel, ladies and gentlemen," announced the driver. "To all who are getting off here, have a great vacation and thanks for traveling with the Tinsel Town Bus Co."

Tugging his lone suitcase from under his seat, Gomez made his way along the aisle. Five other passengers were getting off at this stop.

The eternal midday was pleasantly warm. Gomez whistled as he crossed the pictorial paving and entered the lobby.

It was cool and shadowy and appeared to have an intricately patterned mosaic tile floor, a splashing marble fountain and ceiling beams of sturdy redwood.

"Gomez," he informed the polished silvery robot desk

clerk. "I have a reservation."

The clerkbot was wearing a shirt decorated with animated jungle landscapes. "I noticed you admiring our lobby, sir," he said as he consulted his computer terminal. "You'll be interested to know that it's all an illusion, created by the clever use of holograms and special effects. It's just about nearly one hundred percent fake."

"*Bueno,*" said the detective, smiling, "this sounds like my sort of place."

Wolfe Bosco gestured expansively, waving a hand at the immense swimming pool. "My star has risen, Gomez. I am no longer the pathetic schlep that you encountered a few weeks ago down in the other Hollywood."

"Why, gee, you even have new hair."

The small talent scout stroked the hair at his temple. "I look terrific as a blond," he explained. "When you lunch at an exclusive place like the Poolside Lounge, you're obliged to appear at your best."

Gomez observed, "You also have far fewer wrinkles than when last we met."

"Exactly. The larger the salary, the fewer the wrinkles." He rested an elbow on the small white tabletop. "So, Gomez, how can I be of service to you?"

Gomez was scanning the forty-some tables that circled the sunlit outdoor pool. Every one was occupied, and behind the rows of tables were a dozen small wooden cabañas for those who favored some privacy for their dining. "I hear, from the first chap I contacted after arriving at this sundrenched paradise, that you're still not above peddling information, Wolfe."

The diminutive agent rested his other elbow on the table. "Since I landed my top client, Jacko Fuller, a fat picture deal, I've cut back on some of my other activities," he confided. "Still, for old time's sake *and* a nice big fee, I'll be happy to lend a hand." He paused to wave at a passing blonde. "Hiya, Linda. That's Linda Turner, Jacko's costar in *Love Me Forever.* It's lensing right now over at Galactic Studios."

"I'm truly impressed, Wolfe, at the way you've been able to sell that rundown android replica of a washed-up second-rate singer to these—"

"Shush! Ixnay, Gomez." He slapped his palm over Gomez's hand, shook his blond head warningly and then took a very careful look around at the adjoining tables. "Don't go spreading nasty rumors like that about my number-one client." His voice had dropped to a near whisper.

Gomez laughed. "Ah," he said, "you haven't informed any of these moguls that your Jacko isn't actually a human being."

"Everybody who runs the movie business is young, extremely youthful, Gomez," Wolfe quietly informed him. "They, not a one of them, don't remember the original Jacko Fuller. They think my boy's the real thing. Hell, I could never get the kind of money they're paying for him if they were wise he's an andy sim. So let them, callow schmucks that they are, go on thinking he's the genuine article."

"Serves 'em right," agreed Gomez. "Now about our negotiations?"

"I was a schmuck to admit my little con," sighed the agent ruefully. "You're probably going to hold that over me as we talk fees."

"Nope, Wolfe, I'm going to be extremely generous—in spite of the fact that I can screw up your present and future career. $200."

"$200? Am I hearing correctly? No, I can't be." He patted his wrinkle-free cheeks with his palms. "That's an insulting sort of . . . And yet, it's not all that bad. I'll take it, especially, Gomez, since you happen to have me by the goonies."

"You know Sheldon Gates, don't you?"

"A goniff, but, yeah, I do, alas," said the agent. "Ran into him a few times down on Earth."

"Is he here?"

"You mean at the Poolside Lounge? Naw, this is too high class a hangout for the—"

"Here on New Hollywood."

Wolfe twisted in his seat to watch a slim, tanned blonde young woman make a perfect dive into the pool off the high board. "Too bad her tits are too small for longterm stardom," he commented. "Yeah, Gomez, I seem to have heard that Sheldon made a rather hurried departure from Greater LA and is currently holed up on this satellite."

"Is he residing with his dear old mom?"

"I believe he is indeed in residence with that old yenta."

"Would that be at her place of business—Madame Sonja's Longevity Lodge?"

"That's the place, sure. A very successful scam, so I

hear," answered the agent. "It's over on Rodeo Drive in a building that's shaped pretty much like my Aunt Dorothy's backside."

Gomez told him, "What I need, Wolfe, is a safe and successful means of getting in and out of there. Further, I want to know *exactly* where Shel is located within the establishment."

"That'll cost you $400 extra."

"$200."

"$350."

"$300."

"Okay. It's robbery, but what can I do?" He raised his eyes to the clear sunlit midday sky above. "I'll get you everything you need to know by not later than supper time."

In order to take his leave from the Poolside Lounge, Gomez had to walk by a row of the private dining cabañas.

He was wending his way over the mosaic tiles, circling squat potted palms, when he became aware of some kind of fracas taking place in one of the small wooden buildings. Crockery smashed within, then something hard slammed against one of the opaque windows.

Slowing, Gomez eyed the cabaña as he passed it.

Another piece of dishware smashed within. Then a young woman cried out, "This, and I'm really very ashamed of you, isn't what I came here for!"

A man chuckled in a nasty way. A table fell over with a rattling thunk.

Gomez stopped, looking at the red door.

None of the diners at the nearby tables were paying a bit of attention to the noisy conflict.

Inside the cabaña the woman screamed.

Sighing, Gomez sprinted to the door and caught the handle. He turned it, yanked the door open and went diving inside.

19

THE DAY HAD barely begun, the morning light was thin and tinged with grey. Roger Zangerly yawned twice as he hurried along the plastiglass connecting tube that linked the Mechanix International storehouses in the Oxnard Sector of Greater LA.

Outside, across a stretch of fenced beach, the dawn Pacific was choppy and topped with grey froth. A few gulls were skimming low over the water, the sound of their cries was kept out by the tube walls.

Roger yawned again, saying to himself, "I'm a damn idiot to risk nosing around here."

At the entry portal to Storehouse 3, a gunmetal robot in a khaki suit stood, arms folded across his chest. When Roger was still ten feet from him, the guardbot made a loud clicking sound. His ball-head swiveled, he gazed directly at the approaching man. His eyes glowed, momentarily, green. "Good morning, Mr. Zangerly," the robot said. "Up early, I note. What brings you to our sector of Greater LA?"

"Just routine." Roger handed the robot a blue plasticard. "I need to check on some mothballed andies in Compartment 22. Here's my authorization."

The robot accepted the card, inserting it into the slot in his forehead. After nine seconds, he said, "Okay, you can go in, sir. By the way, the canteen will commence serving breakfast at 6:30 A.M., in case you find yourself feeling hungry after your chores are completed."

"Thanks, that's a good idea." He smiled at the guardbot as he walked by him and into the vast, multiroomed Storehouse 3.

Roger had, very slyly, gone rummaging through the Mechanix files after his brother had phoned him yesterday. He had a fairly high security clearance and, over the years, he'd learned several ways to outfox the company computers. As a consequence, he'd managed to access some information that he wasn't actually supposed to access. He found out that Mechanix had put something called Project Doppelgänger in motion nearly two years ago. There weren't too many details in what he'd dug up thus far, yet sufficient to convince Roger that some android dupes had been built and kept secret.

Some of them, and this involved guesswork as well as facts unearthed, were quite probably being kept here in Storehouse 3 in Compartment 26. Roger decided he wanted a firsthand look.

The air in the metal corridors was chill and didn't

feel like real air when you breathed it. Roger coughed into his hand as he turned a corner.

He ignored Compartment 22 and kept on to 26. The electrokey he'd borrowed last night should open all the doors in this section of the storehouse.

He stuck the key in the slot of the door and it slid silently aside. As Roger crossed the threshold, harsh, yellow light filled the big, metal-walled room.

"Damn," he exclaimed.

Sitting in an armchair on his left was Alicia Bower.

Although Gomez had recognized the young woman's voice, he went shoving on into the dining cabaña anyway. If you were dedicated to practicing chivalry, he figured, you couldn't be selective about it.

The slim, redheaded young woman was standing, widelegged, next to the toppled lunch table. She held a wine flask by its neck and was glowering at the handsome, tanned man, who was sitting cautiously on the floor and rubbing at a fresh bruise on his handsome forehead.

She said, "I assumed, Mr. Meech, that I'd made it perfectly clear that despite the unfortunate fact that I have been temporarily forced to work in, as it were, the salt mines of broadcast journalism, I'm not at all interested in any sort of cheap romantic— Oh, hello there, Gomez."

He gave her a lazy salute. "Greetings, Natalie."

Natalie Dent looked down at the flask in her hand, then let it drop to the dish-strewn floor. "I don't imagine I'll have to bop Mr. Meech again to calm him down,

Gomez, but it's nice to have you standing by, even though you're looking a lot older and flabbier than when I saw you last, since you are very good at knocking bullies and lechers on their respective keesters."

"I am good at that, *sí.*"

From the floor Desmond Meech asked him, "Do you know this hellcat?"

"I must admit that I do," answered the detective. "We're long-time chums."

"She's verbose," remarked the actor.

"That doesn't justify your attacking her."

"This feisty young lady simply doesn't understand the basic ground rules of the show business interview, Mr. . . . Gomez, was it?"

"This is Sid Gomez." Natalie brushed at the skirt of her suitdress. "He happens to be, unless they've finally come to their senses and bounced him, an operative with the prestigious Cosmos Detective Agency."

"Wait now, we don't need any detectives on the scene," said Meech. "I was merely, as I've been attempting to explain since you overturned the damn table on me, being friendly in the venerable show business interview tradition. I assure you, Gomez, that putting my hand on Miss Dent's knee was purely a gesture of avuncular friendship."

"For an actor who's portrayed a doctor on a vidwall show for the past three seasons," remarked Natalie disdainfully, "you certainly have a lousy knowledge of anatomy. That most certainly wasn't my knee that you were attempting to fondle."

Gomez inquired, "Is that your vidcam lying on the floor yonder, Nat?"

"Yes, I dropped it when Meech made his second lunge."

"Interviews are supposed to be like that," persisted the fallen actor. "Some questions, some lunging."

"Gather up your effects, *querida,*" suggested Gomez, "and I'll escort you to safety."

"Any lady is perfectly safe with me," assured Meech. "Have you ever watched my 'Surgeon Stone' show, Gomez?"

"Once."

Natalie retrieved the camera. "I appreciate your barging in, Gomez," she said. "It's nice to have some backup in situations such as this, even though I feel perfectly capable of defending myself against this aging philanderer. Afterall, a man who's pushing fifty isn't that—"

"I'm forty-three," corrected Meech, who was remaining on the floor. "Didn't you read the bio the studio sent you?"

"You couldn't possibly, if you'll pardon my pointing it out, have done that much damage to yourself in a mere forty-three years, Meech." She stepped out into the perennial sunlight.

"By the way," called the actor, "when's the interview going to air?"

"Adiós." Gomez followed the redhaired reporter outside.

She was walking slowly, camera pressed to her chest, toward an exit from the Poolside Lounge. "This is very disheartening."

"You have to accept the fact that some *hombres,* especially those with low standards, are going to find you attractive," he consoled her. "In your line of work that means that—"

"Oh, quit acting like a bigger dimwit than you are," she said, sniffling. "I'm not at all upset over that oafish vidactor. I'm chagrined at your having come across me in this sorry, shabby state."

"You don't look any sorrier or shabbier than usual, Nat."

She sobbed once as they reached the street. "Where are we?"

"Is this a geographical or a metaphysical query?"

She pointed forlornly at the nearest palm tree. "New Hollywood! Good gravy, if you'll excuse my slang, here I am, once one of the biggest and brightest investigative reporters that Newz ever had. My reports brought a new dimension to vidwall muckraking. I've been presented the Lemac Award twice thus far, which isn't bad for a newswoman of twenty-seven."

"Aren't you with Newz anymore?"

"Oh, yes, I'm still working for them," she said, sniffling and sobbing. "But I'm on their black list just at the moment, I'm in the dog house, I'm pounding a beat in the sticks, relegated to sweeping out the stables. It's really—"

"I'm sure your fall from grace makes for a fascinating tale, Nat," he cut in. "But I have a busy agenda ahead of me and—"

"Then you didn't know about my disgrace?"

"Hadn't heard, nope."

"I'm now the host, and it pains me to reveal this to you, Gomez, on 'Show Biz Today.' " She paused, wiped tears from her eyes. "And do you know why this awful fate befell me? Well, I'll tell you exactly how I came to—"

"Better not if it's going to cause you any further stress, *cara*. No, we'll just end this sad conversation right here and now and I'll get on about my business."

"Your business?" She sniffled once more, straightened up, looked him directly in the eye. "That's it! Yes, you, Gomez, flawed vessel that you are, will be my salvation."

"Not if it's going to take more than another five minutes."

"I got shipped up here, four and a half long, dreadful months ago, because one of my hardhitting reports stepped on the toes of a powerful crony of a big-shot Newz exec," the reporter explained. "Ah, but if I could bring in a really terrific scoop, why then—"

"Natalie, my pet, I'm sorry to disappoint you, but I'm here on New Hollywood to look into a very ordinary, very routine matter. It involves just a minor actor whose wife wonders what he's actually—"

"Which actor?"

"Elmo Hess."

"He's not even here. He left for the Moon Colony two weeks ago to start shooting 'Space Devils Fly High.' "

"Oops, then I better rush off and book passage for the Moon. So long."

She caught his arm and held tight. "Please, Gomez, you know full well that I'm not the sort of person who enjoys pleading for a favor, but, please, help me out," she said. "If I can turn in a big story, then I can go over the head of that nitwit exec who exiled me to this limbo and insist that the other Newz bosses reinstate me if they want the rights to the scoop."

"I'm late for an appointment." Smiling guilelessly, he pulled free of her clutch. "But, I swear on my honor, we'll meet for dinner at my hotel tonight at eight. Then I'll give you all the exciting details of the case I'm actually at work upon."

"What hotel are you staying at?"

"The LaBrea Arms," he lied and, turning on his heel, made his getaway.

20

WHEN JAKE AWAKENED two hours earlier, he'd found himself occupying a small rectangular room. Three of the walls were grey and blank, the fourth contained an animated mural depicting a vast field of rippling wheat. Every ten minutes a speaker imbedded in the wall announced: "This detention cell is made possible by a grant from Farmboy Industries—Feeding America from the heart of Farmland."

There was a cot, a chair and a toilet in the detention cell. Jake was pacing now, eyeing the wall where he suspected the door must be.

Three crows, black spots in the sky, flew over the sea of ripe wheat.

"This detention cell is made possible in part by a grant from Farmboy Industries—Feeding America from the heart of Farmland."

"So I've heard," muttered Jake.

The wall he'd been watching produced a sudden purring sound. A panel slid aside, admitting a tall, black-enameled robot and then closing again.

The robot had *Jail Staff* stenciled in white across his polished ebony chest. "Good afternoon, Mr. Cardigan."

"It's afternoon, huh? Same day?"

"The gas used to calm rioters usually pacifies criminals for from five to six hours. It's perfectly harmless, causing no serious side effects in most—"

"Whoa," suggested Jake. "I'm neither a rioter nor a criminal. If you'd allow me to fetch a lawyer, we can—"

"There's no need for that, Mr. Cardigan." Seating himself on the cot, the robot opened a panel in his side. From it he withdrew a sheaf of faxpages. "Although you do have a criminal record, we—"

"Wrong again," interrupted Jake. "I was in prison, but I later received a full pardon."

"I can see you're something of a jailhouse lawyer, Mr. Cardigan." The big black bot produced a hollow chuckling noise deep inside. "I'll have to watch my words more carefully than I do with our average criminal."

Jake grinned thinly. "Exactly what charges am I being held on?"

"You're not being held, Mr. Cardigan."

"Detained then."

"Technically you're not being detained."

Jake pointed a thumb at the mural. "Wall's been telling me for the past two hours that I'm in a detention cell."

"That's simply because our infirmary is full up," explained the staff robot. "This was the only space in the jail complex for you to sleep off the aftereffects."

"Now that I'm wide awake, can I go?"

The robot made the chuckling noise again. "Just as soon as we take care of some necessary red tape," he said. "You're required to answer a few simple—"

"Who requires that?"

"The law in Farmland isn't as loose and sloppy as it is out in Greater Los Angeles, Mr. Cardigan," the robot informed him. "Well, let's get rolling, shall we? What is the true purpose of your visiting Topeka Complex?"

"Vacation," answered Jake.

"And why would a private investigator with one of the nation's leading detective agencies want to vacation here?"

"I've been asking myself the same darn thing," admitted Jake. "But before Farmboy Industries gassed me, I had the notion I could spend a quiet, restful time hereabouts."

"You refuse to state your real reason for being in the area?"

"I just stated it. Pay attention."

"Refuses to answer." The robot checked a box on the top sheet with the electropen built into his forefinger. "The next question has to do with how long you intend to remain in the Topeka Complex."

"Not long."

"Can you be more specific?"

"No more than another week."

"I'm afraid, Mr. Cardigan, that a stay of such duration isn't possible for you."

"Why is that?"

"It's the policy of the Topeka Complex Local Police to move out all undesirables and agitators within forty-eight hours from the time of—"

"Which am I?"

"Neither, yet you do happen to fall under the provisions of the statute." The robot rested the pages on his ebony knee. "I feel that I ought to warn you that if you continue to respond in this negative manner, you may cause your jail release to be delayed."

"Then I'm not really free to go?"

"You are, certainly, provided you first fill out these simple forms in a manner that satisfies—"

Something started banging on the hidden door. After a half dozen thunks, it slid open again. A black young woman came striding in. "Don't say anything else to this junkheap, Cardigan," she advised. "I'm your attorney."

The robot popped to his feet with a clang. "Miss Petway, you happen to be intruding on an official—"

"Scan this, pinhead." She shoved a crinkly sheet of real paper at him.

"An Unconditional Release Order?"

"Very good, you got it right on the first try." She nodded at Jake. "My name's Georgia Petway. We can go."

"Who hired you?"

"Joe Chatman, of course. Most of your other buddies in Farmland are much too chicken to go up against Farmboy." She stepped over to the open doorway. "We'll gather up your belongings, see how many they've tried to swipe, and then shake off the dust of this shithole."

He followed her into the grey corridor.

The wall said, "This detention cell is made possible in part by a grant from Farmboy Industries—Feeding America from the heart of Farmland."

21

"YOU AWARE OF those assholes?"

"The ones tailing us in the grey skycar?"

"That's the very assholes I mean."

Jake nodded. "They picked us up as soon as we departed the hoosegow."

Georgia said, "I suppose I could do some fancy skywork, ditch them."

"You know who they are?"

"They're cops." She was sitting slightly hunched in the driveseat of her crimson skycar. "They're still interested in you—are anxious for you to leave Topeka soon as possible."

"They must know Joe Chatman's the one who brought you into this."

"You mean that even if I cleverly elude these motherhumpers, they'll just hop over to Joe's and wait for us there?"

"Seems logical, yeah."

"You really would have been impressed by my tricky flying, but, okay, let's save everybody's time and fly direct to Joe's."

Jake grinned. "I'm already sufficiently impressed by you," he assured the attorney. "You sprung me out of that detention cell very smoothly."

"That was easy. I've been outfoxing the local cops for years."

Jake observed, "This smells like a company town."

"Sure, but it's more complicated than that." They were flying over the twilight city and she was guiding the skycar deftly through the heavy air traffic at their designated level. "Farmboy Industries is owned—though nobody's been able to prove it, not even Joe—by the biggest Tek cartel in Farmland. Until a few months ago that cartel was, I'm near certain, controlled by a supposedly legit business mogul named Bennett Sands. Then he up and—"

"Got killed," supplied Jake. "I know, yeah. Who runs the cartel now?"

Georgia snapped her fingers, glancing over at him. "Hey, that's right. You're the guy who killed Sands, aren't you? It was on the news."

"Whoa," cautioned Jake. "I was there when Sands got knocked off. As a witness, however, not as the perpetrator."

"But he and your wife were fooling around? I got that part right, don't I?"

"Ex-wife," he said. "Now can we get back to local color?"

"I'm not trying to piss you off, Jake, but Joe gave me the impression you didn't go in for too much bullshit in conversation. So I figured—"

"Okay, sorry. I'm probably still touchy about the subject of my onetime wife and Bennett Sands," he admitted. "Who runs his cartel now?"

"That's uncertain, since a couple of different factions are still contending for control."

Leaning back in the passenger seat, he watched the dozens of skycars rushing through the fading day. "What about the Mentor Psych Centre? Are they tied in with—"

"You really are an outlander." She punched out a landing pattern on the dashpanel. "Around here, most everybody knows that the money that set up Mentor some twenty years ago came from Farmboy. The joint's been extremely profitable, especially because of some of the dubious services it offers its customers."

"For instance?"

"Joe can tell you a lot more than I can, because he's been doing research on the life and times of Dr. Isaac Spearman."

"Spearman runs Mentor, doesn't he?"

"Runs Mentor, sits on the board of Farmboy, is a wonderful person and a real asset to Topeka Complex. Or so one frequently hears on the Farmboy-controlled local media," she said. "Here we are."

Her skycar was settling down on the rutted rooftop landing area of a six-story apartment building in the middle of a block of similar buildings. The streets below had a neglected, rundown appearance. Lights were showing at only a scatter of windows.

"Thanks for springing me." Jake stepped clear of the landed car.

"You ain't absolutely free and clear yet, but I'm working on it," Georgia said. "Our tail's landing over there on the roof of that gutted hotel. Want to wave to them?"

"Nope, that would spoil their fun. I appreciate the lift."

"You'll find Joe down in 4C," she told him. "His guardbots are expecting you, so it's not likely either one'll shoot you." Smiling, she shut the door and then took her skycar up into the gathering dusk.

A wide, white-enameled nursebot was helping Barry Zangerly back into bed when his brother came pushing into his room.

"Take a hike," Roger advised the robot.

"Sir, there are certain rules of behavior that should be adhered—"

"That's okay." Barry disentangled himself from the nurse and sat on the edge of his bed. "He's my brother."

"Kinship certainly doesn't excuse—"

"Out with you," urged Roger, making a shooing motion. "We're going to have a private conversation."

"I'll be within hailing distance, Mr. Barry, in case he gets violent." Sniffing twice, the robot nurse left the large offwhite room.

"Well?" Barry asked as his brother sat down in the wicker chair. "Did you find out something about Alicia?

You must have or you wouldn't be—"

"Hold it." Rising up again, Roger glanced toward the door. From his pocket he drew out a small bug-detector. "Let me sweep this place first."

"C'mon, Rog, nobody is listening in on us." He watched his hefty brother check out the room for eavesdropping gear. "Don't be idiotic."

"Just shut up for another minute or two, huh?"

"Do you know where she is?"

Instead of replying, Roger eased over to the door.

The nursebot had stationed herself just outside. "Am I wanted?"

"Not by us, sweetheart. Move along now." Shutting the door, he returned to the chair.

"Are you satisfied that—"

"Yep, the room isn't bugged," he said. "But there sure is something odd going on. Thing is, brother dear, I'm damned if I can figure out exactly what it is."

"Tell me about Alicia. Do you know where they've got her?"

"Nope." He shook his head, causing the wicker chair to creak. "Haven't the faintest idea. But I can sure tell you where the android dupe is."

Leaning, Barry took hold of his brother's arm. "Then Cardigan was right," he said, inhaling sharply. "What did they use it for?"

"Keep calm," advised Roger. "Far as I can tell, this dupe—which looks exactly like her, down to the last freckle—was built approximately fifteen months ago."

"That's about the same time she was away at the Mentor Foundation."

"Yeah, just about, Barry. The andy is kept in one of our warehouses in the Oxnard Sector. But twice in the past week it was activated and checked out."

"Who? Who used it?"

"Fellow named Rob Stinson, who works for Mechanix as a Vice President in the Oxnard facility."

"What's this Stinson say about why he—"

"Stinson, as of yesterday, is on an extended vacation leave," answered Roger. "And, strangely enough, I haven't located anybody who knows where he's gotten to."

Barry frowned. "They must've used that damned android dupe to plant a false trail, Rog," he said. "Which has to mean that—"

"I agree, something very unusual is happening." Roger coughed into his fist. "Well, I'm going back to my office to do some further digging. I wanted you to know what I'd found out so far."

Barry caught his arm again. "Wait—you sound sort of funny. Is there something else you know that you're keeping back?"

"Well, yes, in a way." Slowly, he stood up. "I was able to poke into the wandering Stinson's message records. In the past week or so he had five vidphone calls from Dad."

"No, Dad can't be involved in any plan to hurt Alicia," Barry insisted, shaking his head.

"Maybe not." Roger shrugged. "I'll find out."

"Then I better tag along." He started to get up.

Roger pushed him, gently, back to a sitting position. "You're not ready to leave here yet," he warned. "Stay in bed and recuperate. I can handle things."

"Don't go barging in, the way you usually tend to do, and accuse our father of kidnapping Alicia."

"All I intend to do, in my best executive manner, is find out what the bloody hell has been going on," he promised. "Trust me."

22

JOE CHATMAN ASKED, "Well?"

After a few seconds Jake answered, "I'm not the best one to give advice on how to lead an exemplary life."

The black man said, "Georgia says it's because I'm still looking for pity."

"She's a very direct person."

They were sitting in the newsman's small, uncluttered parlor, Jake in the windowless room's only armchair, Chatman in his silvery wheelchair.

"Has been awhile," admitted Chatman. "I could be, you know, fitted for legs."

"Do it when you feel ready."

"I might never feel ready."

Jake said, "Suppose we switch back to my problems for awhile?"

"Sure, sorry." He touched a button on the arm of his chair and came rolling nearer to Jake. "First off, Sharon

Harker's legit. I did suggest that she contact you."

"So you don't think she set me up, huh?"

"No, I don't, but there's no way to be sure right now," he said. "She and her kid don't seem to be around anyplace. I got some people hunting, though."

"Someone grab her, or is she hiding out?"

"I'm afraid, Jake, it's the former."

"Who else knew she was going to get in touch with me?"

"I did, she did," answered Chatman. "I didn't confide in anybody."

"Did she give you details about what she knew?"

"Only that there was something going on wrong at the Mentor setup, something that bothered her," he said. "When you showed up, I suggested that Sharon talk to you. She'd heard of you and was impressed by—"

"Hell of a lot of good it did her."

"Jake, hey. Every time a lady gets in trouble, it ain't your fault."

"How long ago was it she told you she was uneasy about something at the center?"

"Few days."

"That's since Alicia Bower disappeared, so this could tie in with her."

"Sharon didn't come right out and say so, but I'm near sure that it must."

Jake leaned forward. "I'm going to have to get inside that place, Joe."

"A very tough thing to accomplish. Dr. Isaac Spearman runs a very secure—"

"Damn it, I'm going to see Chatman!"

Someone had started yelling out in the hallway.

A robot guard warned, "Buddy, stand back or we'll use force to—"

"Chatman! You son of a bitch, where is she?"

"Watch it now, buddy."

"Where's Sharon Harker?" A fist hit the door. "Where is she, damn you!"

Chatman nodded at the door. "Maybe this is somebody we ought to meet."

Getting up, Jake moved to the door. "Yeah, sounds like," he said.

The frail, greyhaired woman reached out, very carefully, to touch the edge of the doctor's huge offwhite desk. "No one has been able to help him," she confessed in a faint, faraway voice.

Dr. Spearman smiled. "That's because no one has truly tried, Mrs. Emers." He was a plump, pink man of fifty and his curly hair and crinkly beard were a golden blond. "But here at the Mentor Psych Centre we're most certainly going to try." He left his offwhite chair, walked around his large desk and stood beside the pale young man who was seated, hunched in on himself, next to Mrs. Emers. "And I can assure you that your son is going to want to help, too. Aren't you, Norby?"

The pale young man glanced up, smiling wanly. "Screw you, Doctor."

"Norby, please," cautioned his mother, reaching out and, carefully, putting her hand on his sleeve.

"That's all right," Spearman assured her. "We understand Norby here and he'll find that he can't annoy us or make us angry by—"

"Screw you, Doctor." Lifting the silver ballclock off the desk, Norby tossed it to the floor.

"Or make us angry by his behavior." Ignoring the clock, the doctor returned to his chair.

Mrs. Emers, very softly, began to cry.

Norby stomped on the fallen clock with his foot, five times.

Dr. Spearman smiled. "You've made the wisest decision for your son in bringing him to us."

"It's quite expensive, but we—"

"Time for a little chat, Isaac." Sam Trinity, dressed in a loose-fitting blue suit and wearing a goldplated hand, had come pushing into the office and was approaching the offwhite desk, shoulders up and head thrust forward.

"Just as soon as I've completed this indoctrination conversation with Mrs. Emers and her son, I'll be more than happy to—"

"Ditch them right now, Isaac."

Norby looked at the redheaded government agent. "Screw you, too," he said quietly.

Trinity laughed and took hold of Norby's ear with his metal fingers. "Kid, it's not really very polite to talk nasty to your elders," he advised him.

His golden fingers crackled. The young man screamed in pain.

Norby brought his hand up to his ear as soon as Trinity let go. The flesh was a blistered red all across the lobe. "You hurt me, asshole."

Mrs. Emers put an arm around him. "Dr. Spearman,

who is this man? Why did you allow him to—"

"Lady, unless you want me to fix that scrawny neck of yours the same way," warned Trinity, "you better drag your halfwit son out of here. Quick pronto."

Spearman was on his feet. "I'm terribly sorry, Mrs. Emers," he said. "This is one of our patients—and I'm at a loss as to how he got loose. If you'll take your son into the foyer, I'll have Dr. Weber attend to him."

"His poor ear's burned like a—"

"Get the hell out," urged Trinity.

"I'm having second thoughts about this place, Doctor."

After escorting the woman and her son out of his office, Spearman said, "I won't have you behaving like that and endangering the business end of—"

"Shut up and listen, Isaac," cut in the OCO agent. "You promised me that you'd have Jake Cardigan taken care of. Since you claim to have such enormous influence in these parts, I assumed you were capable of handling the keeping of him quiet and out of my way for at least a—"

"I got him out of the way, Trinity. He was tossed into our local—"

"But he's out now, Isaac. That jig got him sprung within a few hours. Didn't you anticipate something like that?"

"Joe Chatman turned out to have more connections than I expected," admitted the plump doctor. "But let me remind you that you were always free to handle this yourself. I don't quite understand why you didn't just kill Cardigan as soon as he hit the area."

"That wouldn't be a smart move, not yet," said Trinity. "I just want the bastard sidelined for a few days. Killing him might cause too much trouble."

"Don't tell me the Office of Clandestine Operations is afraid of a smalltime private eye?"

"The Cosmos Detective Agency isn't smalltime," he pointed out. "And just at the moment I'd prefer not to annoy them by killing one of their better ops. Further along, maybe we'll have to risk it." He sank down into the chair that Norby had occupied. "How much more time do you need on Alicia?"

"I've already told you, at least three more days. Four would be even better."

Trinity scratched at his red hair with his golden fingers. "Okay," he said. "Meantime, I'll have to come up with another way to distract Cardigan."

The lean, bald man kept on pacing.

Jake took the chair again. "How much did she tell you, Hershberg?" he asked.

Randy Hershberg turned away from him, concentrating on Chatman. "Why did you ever let Sharon get involved with a Tek dealer like Cardigan? She isn't the sort of person who ought—"

"Whoa now." Jake rose. "I'm not a Tek dealer, never have been."

"Oh, spare me the bullshit, Cardigan." He scowled at him. "I've heard all about you—hell, you did time up in the Freezer."

"Jake was framed," Chatman reminded him. "And he got a complete pardon—eventually."

Jake took hold of the man's shoulder. "Let's," he suggested, "concentrate on Sharon."

"Where do you get off calling her by her first name? You don't even—"

"Listen to me," said Jake evenly. "We all want to find her, but accusing Joe and me of—"

"Chatman convinced her she was some kind of god damn crusader. She'd helped him out before, raising funds, getting petitions signed. Then this mess at Mentor came up and instead of minding her own damn business, she let him convince—"

"Do you work at Mentor?"

"No, at the Prairie. That's how we met and, after her divorce, we—"

"How much did she tell you about what was happening at Mentor?" Jake asked him.

Hershberg shook free of Jake's grip. He circled the wheelchair, stopping behind Chatman. "You know, there's somebody else who should've minded his own business, too."

The newsman frowned up at him. "Who you talking about?"

"Her other great friend—Mel Winter. *Doctor* Mel Winter."

Left eyebrow rising, Chatman told Jake, "Winter works at the Centre."

"And how does he figure in this?"

Hershberg gave an impatient grunt. "He's the one who got Sharon interested in this mess, told her about what was worrying him," he said. "I think—I think Winter even must've showed her some things while she was there. That's what got her so upset, made her come running to Chatman here. A really dumb thing for her to do."

Jake said, "You and the lady don't seem to share an outlook on life."

"I've stuck with her through a lot of rough times," the lean man assured him. "And while I'm not a trouble-maker like your pal Chatman, I do hold decent, liberal opinions. The thing is, the thing I kept trying to explain to Sharon—you can believe in something but not get yourself killed over it."

"Yeah, that's safer," said Chatman.

"Shit, c'mon. You know just about this whole state is controlled by Farmboy," said the angry Hershberg. "Sharon was dependent on them, same as I am. So it just wasn't smart to—"

"Do you think your bosses are the ones who caused her and her son to disappear?" Jake asked him.

Hershberg made an angry, spitting sound. "Hell, no," he said. "I'm not a hypocrite, Cardigan. If I thought that they had anything to do with what's happened to her, I'd go right straight to—"

"But you think it has something to do with Mentor?"

"Yes, even though she never gave me any details."

Chatman inquired, "What do the police have to say?"

"I didn't go to the police, I can't risk that," he answered. "But when I heard the report that she was missing, I decided to come here. Since you—"

"The best thing for you to do is go home and wait."

"That's very tough, just sitting around and—"

"Do it all the same," seconded Jake. "And don't mention to anyone that you told us a damn thing."

23

"*BUENOS DÍAS, POP.*" Gomez went breezing by the robot doorman, giving him a lazy salute, and headed for the backstage area of Ferman's Cinema Palace.

"Just a darn minute, sonny," the chromeplated robot called after him.

"*Sí?*" He halted, shrugged his shoulders slightly and turned to face the movie palace doorman.

"Where the dickens you think you're heading in such an allfired hurry, young fella?"

"Oh, sorry, I should've introduced myself." The curlyhaired detective knuckled his moustache and smiled. "I'm part of Jacko Fuller's entourage."

"Well, then, why didn't you up and say so?" The robot produced a tsking noise as he shook his silvery head. "You people in the show business think you can come waltzing into any old place you please and—"

"My apologies, Pop." Gomez continued on his way. He located Dressing Room 3A, knocked and entered.

Bosco the agent was kneeling on the floor, both tanned hands massaging the knee of the blond, wavyhaired android. "C'mon, kid, give it another try."

"You're making too much of this, Wolfe," the handsome simulacrum told him. "Here's Gomez—let him be the judge."

"Gomez doesn't know his fanny from a barn door."

"Sure, I do. Try me."

The agent urged the android, "Bend your damn leg again, Jacko."

Jacko obliged. "Now ask Gomez for his honest opinion."

"Gomez, meaning no slight, isn't savvy to this sort of nuance." Wheezing slightly, Bosco made it to an upright position. "You did hear it, didn't you, Gomez?"

"Give me some sort of clue."

"The creak," said the agent.

"Beg pardon?"

"The damn creaking his mechanical knee makes."

"Didn't notice it." Gomez shook his head. "Now—about the material you said you'd collected for me."

"See?" Jacko chuckled, pleased. "You're making too much out of this, Wolfe."

Rotating to his right, the agent placed his hands on Gomez's shoulders. "You just wandered in from the outside, right?"

"That I did, *sí.*"

"And what did you notice out there?"

"Several hundred tourists waiting behind a rope."

"Exactly. All of them fans of Jacko's," explained the unhappy Bosco. "Did you also perhaps happen to notice a small rectangle of wet cement?"

"Nope, missed that. Let's get on to what you've gathered for me, Wolfe."

"In a minute." Letting go of the detective, he eased closer to his android client. "Just a few moments from now Jacko will be obliged to go out there and face that clamorous crowd. He must not only put his famous footprints but his handprints as well into that selfsame wet cement."

"This is a real honor for me," put in Jacko, "since the courtyard of Ferman's Cinema Palace is justly famous for its collection of entertainment-world footprints, handprints and—"

"Save the speech," his agent warned him. "The point, Gomez, is that my boy creaks—his damn knee joint makes a loud and distinct metallic creaking sound. When his fans hear that, some of them, as nitwitted as they are, will likely exclaim—'Holy Hannah, this guy's not a human actor, he's nothing more than an old brokedown andy.' Soon as that news gets around, we're finished, washed up."

Gomez told him, "You're making a big fuss over a small noise."

"Ah, then you did hear it?"

"No," lied Gomez. "Shall we get to the information that I came here to pick up from you?"

Shrugging, gazing sadly down at his client's knee, Bosco sighed. From an inner pocket of his flamboyant plaid sportscoat he withdrew a packet. "Sheldon Gates is indeed residing at his dear mother's spa." He handed over the materials. "I got you, among other things, a floorplan of the whole dump, with an X marking the exact suite where Shel is lying low. I'll have to charge you an extra $100 for the map."

"$50." Gomez unfurled the floorplan and slowly eyed it. "And, by the way, what do all these cute little green Xs you've drawn on this represent?"

"Oh, yeah, that's something else I better mention."

"I'd appreciate it."

"By the merest chance, there's a famous actor staying there, too. Incog, doesn't want a soul to tumble to the fact that, at the early age of twenty-two, he's already in need of some serious rejuvenation," the agent explained. "You—"

"Some of them live at such a fast pace." Jacko pursed his lips in sympathy.

"Shut up and limber your knee."

"A little more narration, *por favor,* about these squiggles, Wolfe?"

"Well, those circles, Gomez, represent the extra guards who are stationed at Madame Sonja's Longevity Lodge. They're to keep out the press, fans and similar scum."

Rolling up the plan, Gomez stroked his moustache with it. "Who's the youthful star in question?"

"Carlos Taffy."

"Who's he?"

Jacko chuckled. "Only the hottest teensoap star going," he supplied. "Haven't you ever viewed 'Hotspur Hi'?"

"I keep meaning to, Jacko, but it's always on during the hour I do my homework." Gomez put the papers away, then scanned the ceiling for a few seconds. "A means of access occurs to me—but it's going to call for something drastic."

The agent squatted to tap his client's knee. "You mean violence, Gomez?"

"Only violence to my sensibilities," he answered and took his leave.

Dan Cardigan twisted again in his booth chair. He glanced once more in the direction of the wide doorway to the student lounge. For the fifth time there was no sign of Molly Fine.

She was ten, make that eleven, minutes late so far.

Dan picked up his cup of citriblend, took an absentminded sip, set the cup down again. The lounge, which was called the Squad Room, was located atop the central building of the SoCal State Police Academy. The plastiglass ceiling was tinted a pale blue, and a hard afternoon rain was hitting down on it.

"I'm sorry. Forgive me and so on. Don't take time now to bitch and moan and otherwise complain, because we have something important to discuss." Molly, a slim, darkhaired girl of sixteen, slid into the booth across from him. "I'm here—you can brighten up now, Dan."

"Occupying myself for eleven, make that twelve, minutes with nothing but my thoughts and a cup of fruit punch isn't my idea of—"

"I know how you hate to be separated from me for

even a few minutes, but quit sulking," she advised. "Sit up and pay attention."

"How come you were—"

"I'm late because I was talking on the vidphone."

"That doesn't cheer me up much."

"This was Norm Porter I was talking with."

"The large, handsome suntanned guy you used to date?"

"We've stayed friends," Molly answered, nodding. "What's important for you to grasp is that Norm is presently in the Social Corps. He's stationed down in the Venice Sector."

"That's where Gomez got roughed up."

"You're commencing to comprehend." Molly smiled, reached across the table to pat his hand.

"If you'd come to the point right off, instead of dwelling on the details of your old beau, I'd—"

"My old beau happens to know a girl named Jimalla Keefer," continued Molly. "May I have part of your soy danish?"

"Sure, take what's left."

"Thanks. I don't recall having lunch."

"Damn it, Molly, I keep telling you that you have to eat at regular intervals or—"

"I'm always getting distracted is the problem." She took a bite of the pastry. "Jimalla is a member of the therapy group down there that included Alicia Bower."

"The woman my dad and Gomez are hunting for."

"You told me about the case this morning, so when

Norm—who isn't all that handsome, as a matter of fact, though he's certainly tanned—when he mentioned he knew somebody who knew something about a missing woman named Alicia Bower and was wondering if he ought to tell anyone, I told him to tell me."

"What does he know exactly?"

"Only that Jimalla knows something and is scared," she replied. "Now what we have to do is go talk to—"

"Wait. The last time, Molly, that we teamed up, we came damn close to getting killed."

"You simply aren't taking statistics into consideration, Dan. If you did, you'd realize that the odds are very much against our nearly getting killed every time we investigate something together."

"On top of which, I don't know if my dad would want us to—"

"Didn't he say we made a great team? I heard him myself."

"Maybe I'd better explain irony to you. What he was really—"

"We have a date tonight, don't we?"

"Sure, yeah."

"Okay, since we don't have anything special planned—well, we can go to Venice."

"And see Jimalla Keefer?"

"Norm says he can probably arrange a meeting. Jimalla is scared, but apparently she's also eager to confide in somebody official—and we come close to being official."

"Not that close," he said. "Do we have to see Norm, too?"

Smiling, she held her thumb and forefinger about an inch apart. "Only for a very short span of time," she promised.

"Okay," Dan decided, "we'll go."

24

PAUSING TO CATCH his breath, Gomez scanned the broad lobby of the LaBrea Arms Hotel. Then he muttered, *"Está bien,"* and went trotting across the flowered carpeting toward the robot-staffed desk.

Natalie Dent, a flush commencing to touch her face, was just turning away from one of the white-suited clerkbots. "Suppose, you weasel," said the redhaired reporter on sighting Gomez, "you explain why you're not registered at this hotel?"

Before he responded, the detective struggled a bit more with the contrite expression he was trying to affect. "Ah, I thought perhaps you were confused." He took hold of her arm.

"When people lie to me, even lowlifes as habitually unreliable as you, Gomez, it has a tendency to confuse me, yes," she told him as she retrieved her arm.

"I admit, *chica,* that this misunderstanding was maybe my fault. Afterall, running into you again by chance was such a stimulating surprise that I haven't been thinking as clearly as—"

"Malarkey. You wanted to ditch me, as is often your habit, so you handed me a fake—"

"Were I so eager to ditch you, *cara,* why then am I here dancing attendance on you?"

Natalie halted, placed her hands on her hips and studied him. "It's probable that, after lying to me and sending me on a wild-goose chase, you must've decided that there was some further way you could still exploit my pathetic, naive and illplaced fondness for you."

He denied her accusation with a shake of his head and an injured smile. "Let me be honest with you."

"Ha! That'd be a first."

"I truly, *es verdad,* intended to have dinner with you," he insisted. "But, rattled as I was, I gave you not the name of the hotel I was residing at but rather the name of the hotel where I wanted to take you dining."

"The LaBrea doesn't happen to have a dining room."

"Well, then I was even more rattled than I thought." He caught her arm again, guided her in the direction of a doorway. "The important thing is that I realized my error and rushed over here in time to catch you, Nat. We're together and we'll be able to spend a few precious moments with each other."

"A few moments? Dinner, at least the way I dine, usually takes more than a—"

"I myself was looking ahead to a tête-à-tête of several long, pleasant hours," he assured her as they left the lobby and hit the sunbright street. "I'm assuming, however, that you'll want to go rushing off."

"Why, in heaven's name, would I rush off? Unless, which is, I'm afraid, highly unlikely, I suddenly came to my senses and realized that I was wasting my time and damaging my reputation by being in your disreputable company?"

"Oh, I figured because of the scoop."

"What scoop?"

"The one growing out of the major news tip I'm about to pass on to you," he explained.

The late-afternoon rain was pelting the plazdome that sheltered the wide oval landing area next to Bernard Zangerly's mansion in the Redondo Sector of Greater LA. Roger sat for a moment in his just-landed skycar, gazing absently downhill toward the choppy grey ocean.

Sighing, the husky man eased out of his car. Left eye narrowing, he stood watching his father's house. The low, sprawling home looked especially dark and gloomy this afternoon.

The neowood front door swung open before his foot even hit the first red plaztile step.

"Good afternoon, Master Roger," came a metallic voice from within the shadowy foyer.

Climbing the seven red steps and crossing the threshold, Roger said, "You need a tuneup, Lofting. Anyone over thirty isn't Master anymore."

"You'll always be a lad to me, sir." The butler was an early Mechanix model, nearly twenty-five years old, silverplated and dressed in a crisp black suit. "If I may say so, Master Roger, we don't see you at all often enough these days."

"I wouldn't even be here now, except that Dad apparently left the office early today. Is he all right?"

The old robot tapped his metal chest. "Bit of a cold, sir."

"I have to talk to him."

"You'll find him in his den. I was unable to persuade him to go to bed."

Patting the robot on the shoulder, Roger moved along the hallway to the second door on his left. He halted, knocking.

"Yes, come on in, Rog."

His father didn't look especially well. His thin face had an odd bluish tinge to it and the shadows beneath the eyes seemed deeper than usual. He was sitting behind his desk, stiffly upright in the metal chair.

To the left of the desk was a small bank of monitor screens, one of which offered a view of the front steps.

"You look rotten," observed Roger as he sat in a chair facing the desk.

"Thanks, son."

"Okay, I need to talk to you." He nodded at the bank of small screens. "Turn all that stuff off so—"

"What exactly is bothering you?"

"I'd like privacy before I go on, Dad." From a coat pocket he took the small bug-detector. "If you don't mind, I'll—"

"Well, certainly I mind, Roger." Bernard flicked off the monitors and the screens died. "This room isn't otherwise bugged. Trust me."

Roger hesitated, then allowed the gadget to drop back away into a pocket. "I'd hoped to have a chance to catch you at work," he said. "But maybe this is better."

"Is it Barry? Is your brother—"

"He's fine—fine considering all that's happened to me. But in a way this does have to do with him."

Bernard leaned back in his chair. "I'm actually," he confided, "not feeling all that well."

"Sorry to hear that, but there are some important questions that I absolutely have to ask."

"If this is another quarrel between you and poor Barry concerning Alicia, then perhaps—"

"Actually, Dad, it's about the Alicia android," his son cut in. "See, I've been doing some checking in the Mechanix files and it turns out you're the one who authorized Rob Stinson to activate the Alicia Bower simulacrum that's kept stored at—"

"You don't have access to any of those files."

"Sure, I do." Roger smiled thinly. "Give me credit for knowing a few tricks, huh?"

"But you're absolutely not supposed to go poking into—"

"Let's stick to the point, Dad. Just why did you order this guy to activate that andy? Was it used in some kind of scheme to—"

"Are you saying that your father is involved in—"

"I'm saying that I want to know, have to know, what the hell has been going on," he told him. "Alicia, I realize now, is in some sort of serious trouble. Trouble that has spilled over and already hurt Barry." He rose up out of his chair, jabbed a finger in his father's direction. "Me, I'm aware, you've never much given a shit about. But, hey, I thought you liked Barry. How could you let those bastards work him over?"

"Ah, that's what's really annoying you, isn't it, Roger? Your half-assed notion that I favor him over—"

"Forget that—just tell me about Rob Stinson."

Bernard shut his eyes for a few seconds. "All right, this is the truth," he said, opening them. "Stinson, who has, I might add, now taken off for lord knows where, forged all those authorizations, every damn one of them. He must have had some kind of crooked scheme in mind, possibly to take advantage of Alicia's disappearance, but I have absolutely—"

"Bullshit. You phoned the guy at least a half dozen times."

"Yes, but that was after I suspected that he was up to something."

Roger backed away from the desk, eyes on his father. "You're in on this, aren't you?" he said in a low, rasping voice. "Jesus, I'm not even sure what the hell is in the works, but you know the whole fucking deal."

"I'm not in on a damn thing," insisted Bernard. "You have no right to come here and accuse me, curse me and—"

"Sorry, Dad, but I just don't trust you." He made his way to the door. "But—listen, I'm warning you. I mean to find out what is going on and just what you have to do with it." He turned, left the room and slammed the door.

Bernard shook his head sadly, then nodded up at a spot on the righthand wall. "Did you hear all that?" he asked.

25

SAM TRINITY STEPPED through the bright blue wall. As the panel slid quietly shut behind him, he smoothed the jacket of his creamcolored suit with the fingers of the gunmetal hand he was wearing. The realeather case he was carrying in his other hand rattled slightly as he set it down on the white chair next to the bright orange cot.

Sharon Harker gave a gasping moan, sitting up on the cot. Turning slowly away from the wall, she saw the redhaired OCO agent standing before her. "I'm not," she said in a weak, worndown voice, "going to tell you anything else."

"Sure you are, sweet." Reaching out with his metal fingers, he brushed a curl of blonde hair back from her pale forehead. "Sure you are, so there's no use acting like you aren't."

She tucked her bare legs up under her, pressing her slim back to the bright blue wall. She was wearing only a wrinkled medical gown, bright yellow in color, and it had several stains spread across the front.

Trinity held up his gunmetal hand toward her. "I didn't use this one on you before, hon," he pointed out to her. "This is a brand-new one, far as you're concerned. How are you feeling this afternoon?"

Sharon didn't answer.

Trinity said, "You're an intelligent woman, Dr. Harker. I don't especially like intelligent women myself, even pretty ones like you. But it's my conclusion, based on a hell of a lot of experience, that intelligent women are capable, much more capable than the dumb broads I usually socialize with, of learning from their experiences." Leaning, he spread out the dark fingers of his metallic hand about six inches from her bare knee. "When I ask you a direct question, sweet, I require an answer. Do you remember my telling you that this morning? About how when I asked you something, I expected an answer each time?"

Not looking up at him, she said, "Yes."

"Yes, what?"

"Yes, sir."

"Yes, sir, what?"

"Yes, sir, Mr. Trinity."

"See? That's not too difficult." He lifted his hand from the cot and reached for the realeather case. "I brought you something to look at."

"More hands?"

Trinity smiled. "You also seem to have forgotten that I don't like smartass replies. Did you forget that, Dr. Harker? Did you forget that I don't like smartass replies?"

"I must have."

"Must have, what?"

"Mr. Trinity, sir."

The case gave a harsh, rattling snap as he popped it open. "I brought you a nice picture to look at," said the government agent. "Here, take it."

Very slowly she held out her left hand.

"I didn't know you were lefthanded, Dr. Harker. Are you lefthanded?"

"No."

"No, what?"

"I'm not lefthanded, Mr. Trinity."

"Then why not use your right hand?"

"It's hurt."

"Oh, yeah, I remember now." He gave her the photo.

After she'd looked at it for a half a minute or so, Sharon let it drop to the bright orange fabric of the cot. "You son of a bitch."

"I know, hon, I also warned you about calling me names," he said quietly. "But, hell, we'll let that pass for now. Let it pass because you seem to be upset for some reason."

"What . . . what's wrong with Sean?"

"Is that your son's name? Is his name Sean?"

"Yes."

"Yes, what?"

"Yes, sir, Mr. Trinity, my son's name is Sean. What have you done to him?"

"I haven't done a damn thing to the little darling." He scooped up the picture with his metal fingers.

"He's unconscious in that photo."

"You sure? I think he's maybe only sleeping. Taking, you know, a nap. Kids, little kids, are always snoozing, all the time taking naps." Trinity returned the picture to his case and flipped the lid shut. "I'll tell you where he is, though. Would you like to know where Sean is?"

"Yes, sir, I would."

"He's right here in this very same building. Yeah, little Sean is right here in the Mentor Psych Centre. He's right inside the place you've been so damn curious about, Dr. Harker." Trinity smiled at her. "He's up in the Surgical Wing."

"Surgical? What—"

"They're going to operate on the little guy," he explained. "They're going to try some of what they call exploratory surgery. First on his stomach, then on his chest. Then maybe—"

"What's wrong with him?"

"Nothing at all." Leaning closer, he laughed. "Did you happen to notice that I'm wearing a light suit for this visit?"

"Yes."

"Yes, what?"

"Yes, I saw that you have on a light-colored suit. What does that—"

"If you thought about that for a minute, you'd figure it out," he suggested to her. "You'd probably conclude that I don't do much direct inquiring when I'm dressed like this. The reason for that being that I don't want to get my suit dirty. So I have no intention of doing you any physical harm, sweet."

"It's Sean. You're going to—"

"No, I'm not. But some of Dr. Spearman's people are eager to get to work on little Sean. They want to take a look at some of your kid's insides, see how various new surgical gear will work out. One of these sawbones, not a guy I much care for, has been after me to let him do a side study on how kids can stand pain. I told him I probably wouldn't let him go that far."

"You can't—"

"I can okay anything I want, Dr. Harker. Do you understand the situation you're in?"

"What do you want?"

"I just have some questions, a few more questions."

Her breath exhaled out in a low, sad sigh. "Ask them."

Trinity lifted the case off the chair and sat down. "You told me about Cardigan this morning, about how you intended to meet him," he said. "Now I have to know who your source of information inside Mentor is."

She looked directly at the government agent. "And you won't hurt Sean?"

Trinity's smiled widened. "I'll be much less likely to," he said.

26

A ROBOT FELL over out in the hall. It made a loud, rattling, thunking sound and the wall of Chatman's parlor gave a sympathetic shudder.

Jake jumped to his feet, snapping his stungun out of its holster.

The door clicked several times, then came flapping open.

"Surrender your weapon, please, Mr. Cardigan." The lean black man in the doorway wore a conservative grey suit. In his left hand he held a lazgun, in his right he clutched a sheaf of official-looking papers. "I'm Quincy McCanyon of the Federal Oversight Bureau."

Jake eyed him for a few seconds, then let his stungun fall to the floor. "Why the hell are you busting in on a—"

"If you'll just scan these various forms, Mr. Cardigan, you'll find that I have complete authorization for all my actions."

"McCanyon," mused Chatman from his wheelchair. "Yeah, I heard of this guy. Putz was the term came up most often."

The FOB agent glanced, very briefly, at the newsman. "I've heard a good deal about you, too, Mr. Chatman," he informed him. "Dangerous radical is the phrase most often used to describe you."

Jake had been looking over the assortment of forms. "You intend to take me into custody, McCanyon?"

"There's simply been a request from Washington to question you, Mr. Cardigan," explained the agent, reclaiming the handful of papers. "This, as Order 203/X clearly states, is most certainly not an arrest. We're only escorting you to—"

"Trinity," muttered Chatman, rolling himself over to the doorway to take a look out into the hall. "I'll bet you that redheaded motherhumper is behind this."

"You'd be absolutely wrong there, Mr. Chatman."

"Shit, one of my guardbots is all bunged up, lying there on his tin ass."

"Perhaps you ought to instruct them to respond more quickly to an official entry order," suggested the government agent. "Now then, Mr. Cardigan, if you'll prepare yourself to accompany me."

Chatman shut the door. "You don't have to go with him," he told Jake. "We'll get Georgia Petway over here to throw a spanner in this putz's plans and—"

"My orders can't be set aside," said McCanyon impatiently as he tucked the papers away inside his grey jacket. "Now, Mr. Cardigan, if you'd be good enough to come away with me. Our regional office is—"

All at once his elbows snapped against his sides and his fingers spread wide, his lazgun flipped free and plummeted to the floor.

A beam had come sizzling from the stungun built into the right arm of Chatman's chair and hit the government agent square in the midsection.

As the unconscious McCanyon dropped to the floor, Jake dived and grabbed up the lazgun. "That, Joe, is an extremely efficient chair," he observed, retrieving his stungun and tucking it away.

"Friend of mine helped me modify it some." He touched a spot on the left arm of the chair and a panel in the far wall slid quietly open. "You best get your butt on out of here, Jake. Go down that staircase yonder and you'll come out at street level about a half block from here. Then you—"

"What about him?" He nudged the collapsed FOB agent in the side with his boot toe.

"I got a friend who'll help me get this putz transported elsewhere and kept out of action for awhile," Chatman assured him. "You got Georgia's address, don't you? Get over there and see can she help you to run down Dr. Mel Winter."

"I want to talk to him, yeah. But are you sure you—"

"Age has really slowed you down. Used to be you did more moving and less talking."

While crossing to the opening in the parlor wall, Jake paused to set the lazgun carefully in his friend's lap. "Thanks, Joe. I really—"

"Get going, get going," urged Chatman. "Before more assholes come here looking for you."

27

THE SMALL MAGLEV truck floated smoothly and swiftly through the dimlit tunnel. Natalie and Gomez were sharing the cab with a copperplated robot driver. The bot wore a coverall with *Hedley's Youth Rejuvenator Beam* stenciled across the chest; the redhaired reporter held her vidcam across her knees.

"Explain to me again, since I still fail to comprehend your motives," she was saying.

The detective, who was jammed between her and the bulky truckdriver, replied, "I am merely tagging along to keep you company, *chiquita.*"

"The way you rushed through dinner, I got the impression you couldn't bear to spend much—"

"That's just it. I realized I'd given you a false impression, simply because I was anxious that you be the first show-business reporter to interview the illustrious

Carlos Taffy," he explained. "Therefore, to prove my continuing interest in you, I decided to accompany you. And it'll be educational to watch a crackerjack investigative journalist go after a—"

"Oh, hogwash. Interviewing this vapid adolescent ninny is important to me solely because it'll impress my thickheaded bosses, but it's certainly no great intellectual or reportorial feat."

"The way you quickly arranged to get us into the bowels of this satellite, then rigged a ride in this delivery vehicle bound for the very heart of Madame Sonja's—that impressed me, Nat."

The big coppery robot observed, "I think this doof is handing you a line, sister."

"Concentrate on your driving," advised Gomez.

"The truck takes care of that, bud. I'm mostly along for show."

"It's starting to dawn on me," said Natalie. "What a dolt I am, Gomez, for not seeing to the core of your feeble little ruse before this."

"Eh?"

"Certainly, you have to get inside the spa on the sly and you, knowing that I can be manipulated for your selfish ends, concocted a yarn that would—"

"*Momentito,* Nat," he broke in. "Carlos Taffy *is* residing at the lodge under an assumed name. You established that before you used your connections to arrange our sneaky entry. Therefore, you can't accuse—"

"Oh, yes, that simp is here and I'll do my interview. But you, cunning scoundrel that you are, you have an altogether different motive for accompanying me here."

"Want I should put the slug on him for you, lady?"

"No, it makes me queasy whenever somebody gives him a beating he usually richly deserves."

Gomez assumed a contrite expression. "Well, okay, Natalie," he said in an apologetic tone, "I'll admit that I do have another small reason for wanting to slip inside Madame Sonja's establishment unnoticed."

"Exactly as I suspected. It has, I've no doubt, to do with the case that brought you up here to New Hollywood in the first place. The case that you've been thus far so secretive about."

"It is that very case, *sí,*" he confessed. "You see, *cara,* there's a wellknown civic official from Greater Los Angeles who took off with a satchel full of important infodiscs. They contain information that certain of his colleagues back home don't want to have to buy back from him. I only hours ago learned that he was lying low at the lodge."

"And that's why you wanted me to help you sneak around the guards and security people?"

Gomez nodded. "I didn't tell you earlier, because I feared you'd ferret the lad out on your own and break the story to the world. That would've screwed up me and the Cosmos agency and—"

"Why, Gomez, dear, all you had to do, and I'm really surprised that you haven't realized that about me in all the many years that we've known each other—all you had to do was ask me to lay off the story until you had your man."

"Really? Well, how did I get such a wrong impression of you?"

"While I'm interviewing Carlos Taffy, you go right ahead and apprehend your blackmailer," she told him. "We'll meet back here in this tunnel afterwards. If you're ready to share any details, why that'll be plenty of time for me to file a story and impress Newz, Inc. with the fact that I'm still an ace reporter."

"Terrific, Nat, I'll do just that."

Smiling, she turned on the seat and slipped an arm around his neck. She pulled herself, gently, nearer and kissed Gomez on the cheek. "No hard feelings," she assured him.

"You're making a mistake, sis," said the robot.

The dusty white dog, a small scruffy mutt, was standing wide-legged on a weedy patch of dry lawn at the center of the dimlit courtyard. He was barking enthusiastically at the dented, rattling robot who was attempting to mow the grass.

"Leave me be," complained the battered bot.

On the red plaztile porch of Cottage 3 of the Venice Vista Apartment Court sat a plump young woman in her early twenties. She had a woebegone set of Tek gear, including a dirty Brainbox and a bent headset, arranged on the top step beside her. There was an old unplugged guitar spread across her wide lap and she was laughing at the unhappy robot gardener.

"Norm thinks it's important to live among the people he's working with," explained Molly as she and Dan made their way along the white gravel path that circled the courtyard.

"Beat it, darn you," the robot warned the yapping little mutt.

When the plump woman laughed again, her guitar went falling off her lap.

"Norm's back in Cottage 8."

"I'm wondering," said Dan, tightening his grip on her hand, "how smart it was to come down here."

"This is good practice," she said.

All at once up ahead in Cottage 8 someone cried out in pain.

"Tell us! C'mon, you putz!" shouted someone else.

Letting go of Molly's hand, Dan started running for Norm Porter's cottage.

"Wait now." She ran, too, catching up with him and then reaching under her skirt. "We can use this." Her right hand reappeared holding a small stungun.

"Where'd you get—"

"Watch him, look out!" came another voice from within the cottage.

The door of the place came flapping open. A tall suntanned young man, his face battered and bloody, dived out into the night.

"Norm," gasped Molly.

Another young man, thickset and shaggy, appeared in the open doorway.

"Leave him alone," warned Molly, clutching her stungun in both hands and aiming it up at him.

"Hell with you, bitch." The shaggy young man started to come down the steps.

Then a large hand grabbed him from behind and yanked him back into the house. "Time to go, asshole!"

Norm had managed to come stumbling down the stairs. "They wanted . . . wanted to know where . . ."

"Easy, take it easy." Dan lunged, caught the bloody social worker before he toppled over.

"They want Jimalla," Norm was able to get out before he dropped into unconsciousness.

Roger Zangerly was in an office where he wasn't supposed to be. It was long after closing time and this wing of the Mechanix International complex was quiet and deserted. The night lights made everything seem pale green.

Roger was sitting at a desk he wasn't supposed to be sitting at, using a computer terminal he wasn't authorized to use. He also wasn't supposed to have knowledge of the access procedures he'd used to get at the Security Division files.

"Okay," he was requesting, "give me the current whereabouts of Alicia Bower."

The computer remained silent for nearly ten seconds. Then it said, "May we have your ID code again, please?"

"Sure, it's 1343K-JSG-94702."

"Thank you." Another ten seconds of silence followed. "We have no information on Alicia Bower, sorry."

"Shit." Roger drummed his fingers on the desk top. "Okay, then how about Rob Stinson—where can he be found?"

"Forgive us, but can you repeat your ID code again?"

"I just did that. Why don't you—"

"Once more, if you would, please."

"1343K-JSG-94702. Make a note this time, huh?"

"That's fine," said the metallic voice of the computer. "We'll have your information for you very soon. If you'll just remain right there until—"

"I think not, no." Feeling suddenly uneasy, Roger popped free of the chair and went sprinting for the doorway.

He made it out into the greenlit night corridor beyond and stood listening for a moment. Everything was as quiet as it had been earlier.

But he decided it was time to get the hell out of the building. There had been something slightly offkilter about his encounter with the security computer.

Walking rapidly along the curving corridor, he came to the doorway that led over to his wing of the complex. The thick metal door would no longer open to his touch.

Roger punched out an emergency code on the control panel next to the reluctant door. It still would not slide aside.

He turned, started back the way he'd come. He was running now.

There was another corridor that branched off this one, and the door leading to it opened with no trouble.

He still ought to be able to get himself clear of this damn wing.

But the door at the end of this corridor refused to open.

Roger backtracked.

He found another exit, headed along another shadowy passage.

Another frozen door, another sidetrack.

He stopped finally, leaned back against a pale-green wall. "I'm starting," he admitted to himself, "to get somewhat confused."

He was no longer certain in which direction his part of the Mechanix complex lay.

The corridor he was now in didn't look at all familiar. And there were no signs or direction lights anywhere.

Taking a deep breath, he started moving again.

He located a new doorway on his right. It opened for him.

This was a large, dimlit display room. There were thirteen low pedestals circling the room and on each stood, silent and unmoving, a Mechanix medical robot or android.

"This must be the Medix Wing," he told himself. "So I ought to be able to get back to my office from here."

He started across the room.

"Poor Mr. Zangerly."

He stopped, looking around.

A husky nursebot had stepped off a pedestal and was hurrying toward him. "You don't look at all well."

"Actually I'm fine. All you have to do is point me in the direction of my—"

"You're all feverish."

"That's just from running. It's—"

"What a pity." The big robot caught hold of him. "You'll feel a whole lot better after this shot."

28

YOU COULD SEE the place glowing, a harsh, throbbing red, from blocks away. It covered over two full acres of ground, was built of great panes of flashing plastiglass and resembled a gigantic barn. Floating above it was a huge lightsign that flashed its name—THE BARN—into the surrounding night. At least a dozen skycars were approaching the acre of landing area and land vehicles were rolling into the equally large parking area beyond that.

"Impressive, huh?" inquired Georgia, punching out a landing pattern on her skycar's dash. "Subtle, too."

"Explain this setup a little more," requested Jake.

"The Barn is a sort of entertainment mall for the local sodkickers and faux sodkickers," she answered. "But underneath you'll find a warren of assorted criminal enterprises. Many of them are known to the law, but ignored because of a flourishing system of bribes and kickbacks."

The skycar set down, shimmying slightly, next to a skyvan that had been redesigned to resemble an immense ear of corn.

"And you're sure Dr. Mel Winter is going to be under here someplace?"

"Damn near sure." She climbed free of the car. "When you asked me to get a lead as to his current whereabouts, I asked around. Supposedly the good doctor is here, waiting to get himself shipped out of the country. Apparently he's got a bug up his rear and wants to get clear of Farmland before he disappears like Sharon Harker."

There was noise and music pouring out of The Barn. The entire landing area and the walkways leading to the arched entrances were bathed with a pulsing red by the blazing lights of the walls.

"It's going to be fifty bucks a head," Georgia told him. "You got that much?"

He grinned. "The agency is generous with expense money."

A tall, automated scarecrow stood at the doorway. "Fifty smackers each," it demanded of each customer.

When Jake placed $100 in Banx chits in the scarecrow's gloved hand, it said, "Much obliged, stranger. You and the little lady make yourselves to home."

"Shucks," said Jake.

"We got to head over this way." Georgia took his arm and guided him to the left.

They passed an enormous woodplank dance floor that held several hundred squaredancers. Up on a platform, electrified downhome music was being played by a quintet of big copperplated robots dressed in overalls and straw hats. Painted on the face of the bass drum was *Granpappy Gitfiddle & His Hired Hands.*

As they passed the floor, a heavyset young man took a stumble, fell off onto the walkway in their path. He had *Farmboy Industries—Feeding America from the Heart of Farmland* inscribed across the back of his jacket in globolts.

Bending, Jake helped him to his feet. "That's one of my favorite slogans."

"Huh?" The heavyset youth blinked. "You looking for trouble, outlander?"

"Heck no."

"C'mon." Georgia hurried Jake along. "Don't get into no ruckuses with the yokels."

"Shucks, I was just trying to be neighborly, ma'am."

Great smashing noises were coming from up ahead on their right, along with booming explosions and huge swirls of sooty smoke. The walkway wound by a large, open arena where a sizeable crowd was watching a demolition derby involving a score of antique pickup trucks.

Georgia remarked, "We got quite a night life in these parts."

"So I'm experiencing."

She guided him down a side passway. "We got to go in here first off."

There was a barn within The Barn, a big red structure made of neowood. Over the wide entrance hung a wooden sign announcing HAYLOFT WHOREHOUSE.

"Howdy, folks," greeted the barefooted robot sitting on a bale of straw just to the right of the door. "What can I do ya for this evenin'? We got three under-age virgins—humans I mean to say—along with our usual exceptional run of accommidatin' andies of every gender."

Georgia leaned close to him. "We come on business, Zeke," she told the robot. "The frost is on the pumpkin."

"Ah, I got ya." He tapped the side of his metal nose with his silvery forefinger. "Go right on in, missy, and take the door to the Feed Room. This here young feller with you?"

"Yep."

"Okay, get on in with ya. Too bad, mister, you're on business. We don't get virgins every night, I can tell ya."

Beyond the Feed Room door a dimlit ramp led them down beneath the barn. At the end of that was another door. Passing through that doorway brought them into a long, curving metal corridor.

When they reached the heavy door at the corridor's end, a portion of the wall on their right turned transparent and revealed a small, brightlit room.

A blond young man was sitting in a rocker with a lazrifle resting across his knees. "Yeah?" came his amplified voice.

"The frost is on the pumpkin," called out Georgia in his direction.

"Oaky doaks."

The wall blanked and the door slid open.

The next corridor was longer, narrower and better illuminated. At its end stood a small, pale man in a baggy green suit.

He was shifting nervously from foot to foot. "Evening to you, Georgia dear."

"Hi, Ryder," she said. "So can we talk to Dr. Winter now?"

Ryder shifted from foot to foot a few more times and made a disgruntled noise. "Afraid you're going to have a wait, hon," he told her. "The crazy fool just tried to do the dutch."

"Tried to kill himself?"

"Damned if he didn't. Soon as we finish pumping him out and shooting him up with antidotes, you can give it a try," he said forlornly. "But I can't promise he'll ever be in any shape to talk to you folks."

"Shit," observed Jake.

29

GOMEZ THRUST HIS stungun back away into his shoulder holster. Squatting, he took hold of the disabled grey guardbot by its metallic armpits and dragged it away from the spot behind the high holographic hedge where it had been on duty and into the narrow, quirky alley between the two modest villas.

Approaching the bright green simulated hedge again, he scanned the artificial turf. "*Sin falta* . . . here's the secsystem control panel."

He knelt, took a small tool kit out of his pocket. Deftly he removed the small panel that covered the alarm system controls. In a little less than six minutes he had shut down the whole setup that protected the villa where Sheldon Gates was hiding out.

Pocketing the kit, Gomez eased through the simulated hedge and approached the blank yellow wall of the villa.

As he'd anticipated, the opaque plastiglass door marked SERVICE ENTRY didn't make any warning noises when he jobbed the lock mechanism.

Slowly and carefully he shoved the door open. The aircirc system was pumping a mixture strongly tinged with the scent of wild flowers into the long blank corridor that Gomez stepped into.

He stopped still, stood listening.

". . . an International Drug Control Agency spokesman reports a successful raid on a Tek chip processing plant in the TriState complex earlier today . . ." A deep, slick voice was intoning the news in a nearby room.

Going by the floorplan he'd memorized, the newscast was coming from the lower recroom.

And it seemed likely that the fugitive Shel was in there now, filling himself in on the events of the day.

Gomez remained where he was, bringing his stungun out into the open once again.

". . . the President today signed into law the final Brazil War veterans benefits package . . ."

Nodding, the detective started along the hallway.

He walked silently to the door of the lower recroom. Reaching out with his free hand, he took hold of the handle.

He shoved the panel open and ducked across the threshold, gun ready.

"Greetings from the folks back home, Shel," he said, pointing his stungun at the blond, sunbrown fugitive.

Sheldon Gates had been sprawled in an armchair, watching the vidwall. He was some five feet from the detective.

"Yow!" he exclaimed. Then, somewhat to Gomez's surprise, Gates leaped from his chair, came charging straight at him and butted him hard in the stomach with his closecropped head.

A chill night wind was blowing in across the dark Pacific. The realwood sign dangling from the slanting shingle roof of the Oceanfront People's Clinic was rattling and creaking.

On the cracked sidewalk near the doorway a neon-trimmed robot was hawking soydogs and lentilburgers. "You are what you eat," he croaked, his body flashing crimson, golden, then sea blue.

Skirting him, Dan and Molly entered the clinic.

In the reception room a motherly robot in a flowered apron was sitting in a rocker, embroidering a hand towel. "My gracious, you two lambs are all splattered with blood." The robot jumped to her feet. "Whatever on earth has—"

"It's not our blood," explained Dan. "A friend of ours was beaten up."

"We just came from dropping him at the Emergency Wing," added Molly.

"I think maybe Dr. Moreno can help us," said Dan.

"Well, now, I just bet he can. You poor things wait right here while I fetch the—"

"What's the row about, Moms?" Dr. Harry Moreno came lumbering into the room, a mug of steaming herb tea clutched in his hand.

"Dr. Moreno?" said Dan, stepping toward him. "I'm Dan Cardigan and this is Molly Fine. My father is

Jake Cardigan and he's an operative with the Cosmos Detective—"

"Yeah, I've heard of him. Matter of fact, I was chatting with his partner, Sid Gomez, only—"

"I know. My dad told me quite a lot about this case they're working on."

"Does this mess you seem to be in have something to do with Alicia Bower, too?"

"We think so," answered Molly. "And maybe with Jimalla Keefer."

"Jim? How does she—"

"Here's what's been going on," said Dan and told the bearded therapist why he and Molly had come to the Venice Sector and some of what had happened to Norm Porter.

Molly added, "Norm told us that those goons wanted to know where they could find Jimalla. And they didn't want him or anybody else to talk to her before they found her."

"Damn, sounds like Jim's in trouble again." Moreno scratched at his grey-tinged beard.

"I was hoping, since you know her pretty well, that you might have some idea where Jimalla'd be likely to hide out," said Dan hopefully. "It's important to find her before those guys do."

Nodding, Moreno set the mug down on the reception desk. "I know a couple of places we can look," he told them.

"You shouldn't have bopped me so hard," complained Gates, who was back sprawled in his chair and rubbing at the side of his head. "I was simply manifesting what's known as the Trapped Rat Syndrome. That involves unreasoning panic and an irrational attempt at flight even though the odds are—"

"What say we get down to specifics, lest you next experience the wellknown Boot in the Ass Syndrome?" Gomez, stungun in hand, was perched on the arm of the bright orange plastiglass sofa.

Gates rubbed at his head again, wincing. "The brain, you know, is a delicate—"

"I'm deeply interested in your brain," the detective assured him. "Especially in what it can recall about the events leading up to your rather hasty departure from Greater LA."

"I didn't kill Ford Jaspers."

"Oh, so?"

Shifting in his chair, Gates said, "You're looking at me as though you don't accept my innocence, Sid. That's because, unfortunately, I tend to give off an aura of culpability even when I'm perfectly—"

"So who did knock off the old ham?"

Gates glanced up at the ceiling. "Despite my career, I have a very difficult time snitching on others," he confided. "It goes back, I believe, to an incident in my childhood when my dear mom, through no fault of her own—"

"Who did it, Shel?"

"Well," said Gates quietly, "it was Myra Ettinger."

"The acting CEO of Mechanix International—how did that come about?"

Gates took a deep breath and held it for a few seconds. Sighing out air, he said, "Let me backtrack a bit so that—"

"Not all the way to your childhood again, *por favor.*"

"No, this is about why I joined Dr. Moreno's therapy group," he explained. "You know, it's sad that I didn't get into something like that long ago. I got some real insights into my own tangled—"

"Somebody hired you to sit in, didn't they?"

"Right, yes. That was Myra. She knew . . . well, it shames me some to admit this, Sid, but I have a reputation as an undercover operative and—"

"A spy and a sneak."

"A harsh term, yet apt. Anyway, Myra approached me and arranged for me to get into the same sessions that Alicia Bower was attending."

"And why was that?"

"They wanted to know what was troubling her, what she was talking about in front of the others." He rubbed at his head yet again. "They were afraid she was going to remember something."

"Who's they?"

"Well, it's Myra for certain and a fellow I saw a couple times named Bernard Zangerly. I'm not sure, but I firmly believe it's also her father, Alicia's father. All of them Mechanix people, of course."

"What exactly were they afraid she was on the brink of remembering?"

"I don't know that, Sid. I mean, if they told me what

it was, then I'd know, too, and be as dangerous to them as Alicia was. Right?"

"If she was so dangerous, why not just kill her instead of spying on her?"

"I think Myra would've, but her father wouldn't allow anything like that, you see. He loved her I guess, although parental love, as I know well, can sometimes take strange and quirky turnings as it—"

"What was wrong with the lady's memory—amnesia?"

Gates shook his head. "Well, amnesia in a way, except it had been induced," he said. "At least that was my impression from hints that Myra let drop. Then it started to look, which truly upset them, as though it hadn't taken and she was starting to remember."

"Is that how Tin Lizzie ties in?"

Gates became interested in the ceiling again. "I imagine so, Sid, but I still don't actually know who Tin Lizzie is or what that means."

"Don't you?"

"No, honestly, even though I look to you right at the moment as though I'm lying in my teeth."

"What part does Ford Jaspers play in this mess?"

"It turns out, you know, you can't trust anybody. I should've learned early on, because of things that occurred in my youth, through no fault of my dear mom's, that most people can't be relied on or trusted much. Even so, I accept Ford as a pathetic old hasbeen. Turns out, you know, that he was a longtime blackmailer and—"

"I know about that part. Why did Myra kill him off?"

"That night that he came calling on me, she happened to be visiting me," said Gates, shifting in his seat. "Besides getting regular reports from me about Alicia, Myra . . . Well, sometimes, through no fault of my own, older women seem to become extremely fond of me. Anyway, she was in the bedroom when Ford came to the door. Turns out he'd tumbled to me and had been tailing me. Once Alicia vanished, he figured it was time to try to collect some dough. He knew I'd been filing reports to the Mechanix people and he knew they were worried about something she knew. It was his notion that I was to persuade Mechanix to pay him a hefty sum—the old fool actually wanted $1,000,000—or he'd give what he knew to connections of his in the media. Well, at that point Myra pops out of the bedroom, still jaybird naked, and kills him with her lazgun. Right on my damn floor, if you please."

"Do you know where Alicia Bower is?"

"I don't, Sid, honestly. All I know is that after I reported to Myra that Alicia seemed close to remembering whatever it was that bothered her, they arranged for her to vanish." He touched at the sore spot at the side of his head. "I don't know who grabbed her, how it was done or where she is now."

"Is she still alive?"

"I sure hope so. She was a very nice young woman and some of the things that had happened to her struck a familiar—"

"You, greaseball, drop the gun and quit annoying

my Shelly." A hefty, silverhaired woman of about fifty had appeared suddenly in the doorway. In each plump, beringed hand she held a lazgun.

"Mom," said Gates, "I keep telling you not to call me Shelly anymore."

30

THERE WAS A holographic fireplace in one corner with a heap of blazing logs within it, but the small underground room was damp and chill. Ryder stood at the foot of the brass bed, shifting from foot to foot and now and then glancing back at the doorway Georgia had left by a few minutes earlier.

A fat greyhaired man was standing next to the bed, watching the lean, bald man lying atop the rumpled multicolored quilt. "You'll make it," he said.

"I didn't especially wish to make it," Dr. Winter told him in a quiet voice. "Those capsules I borrowed from the Centre were supposed to—"

"When you're through bitching," said Jake from where he was standing at the other side of the bed, "I want to talk to you."

"Who the devil might you be?" Winter propped himself up on his elbows. "Why have you been allowed to intrude—"

"Jake Cardigan," he said evenly.

"Oh, of course. The aggressive private eye."

"Where's Alicia Bower?"

"Go away, Cardigan. Just tonight I finally made up my mind I can't handle all the stresses and lies of my life," Winter explained to him. "When I fully realized all the harm I've caused, I decided to get myself out of the whole bloody mess."

"You can, far as I care, give it another try soon as I'm gone." Leaning, Jake caught hold of the front of the doctor's shirt and yanked him closer. "Is she inside that damn Mentor setup?"

"Yes, and, please, let go of me, damn you."

Jake held on. "Why is she there?"

"It really doesn't matter, Cardigan," said the psychiatrist. "I thought for awhile that, with Sharon Harker's help, I could finally do something. When that got so fouled up, I figured I could at least get myself free and clear. Get to Europe, hide out there for a time, take on a new identity and possibly work in my field again eventually. But, I don't know, waiting here in this dismal hole, it struck me that I really was better off just—"

"Life's sure sad at times, yeah," cut in Jake, letting go of his shirt. "Let's get back to why Alicia Bower was brought here."

"Actually she was *returned* to the Centre. By that brutal cyborg, Sam Trinity."

Jake sat on the edge of the bed. "How come a government agent is concerned with this?"

"I still don't have all the details, Cardigan. It's my understanding, however, that Mechanix International and the Office of Clandestine Operations have been working together on something very secret and extremely nasty."

"And Alicia found out about that?"

"Exactly, but because she's the daughter of Owen Bower, everyone decided to be gentle with her," he continued. "So she was put in the hands of Dr. Isaac Spearman and . . ." Winter paused, brought one hand up to his eyes and began to cry. "Oh, lord, the things I've been a party to, Cardigan. I went along with it initially, but, when they brought the poor girl back a second time, I simply . . ." He twisted on the bed, tugged a plyochief out of his trouser pocket and wiped at his eyes.

"Spearman worked on her somehow—made her forget all about what it was she wasn't supposed to know?"

"Yes, that was done to her about a year or more ago," he replied. "The trouble is, and that's one of the chief problems with many of Spearman's more experimental electronic therapies, that the cures aren't always . . ." He laughed. "Jesus, I still sound like that bastard. Calling that awful process a cure. At any rate, Cardigan, she apparently started to remember again. That frightened Trinity and certain people at Mechanix. But since she was still the daughter of the head man, no one wanted to silence her permanently." He laughed again. "The humane thing, they decided, was to ship her back to Spearman and let him have another try."

Jake asked him, "And who's Tin Lizzie?"

Dr. Winter frowned at him. "That's the nickname of one of the robot nurses in the Restraint Wing, which is where Alicia is. How did you—"

"We got trouble, folks," announced Georgia, popping into the chill room.

Jake stood clear of the bed. "What's wrong?"

"Some OCO agents have been spotted upstairs," she answered. "It's likely they'll head down here eventually."

"We'll have to move Winter," said Ryder. "And get ourselves the hell out of here, too."

"Not before," said Jake, "I ask him a few more questions."

Madame Sonja, both lazguns still trained on Gomez, had moved over beside her son's chair. "That bump looks awful," she was saying. "Are you absolutely sure, Shelly, that he didn't hurt you seriously?"

"Mom, he just bopped me on the coco with his fist. I'm okay, truly."

"In your offspring's line of work, *señora,*" mentioned Gomez, who had dropped his stungun and raised his hands, "physical harm is one of the occupational hazards."

"You've got a hell of a nerve, greaseball," the spa owner told him. "You break in here, hurt my Sonny Boy and then—"

"Mom, hey, what did I tell you about using Sonny Boy in front of visitors?"

"This shlunk isn't a visitor, he's an intruder—one step away from a burglar."

"Line of duty," suggested Gomez. "Your Sonny Boy here happens to be a fugitive from the law, ma'am. Which means that private detectives, police officers, bounty hunters and the like are going to feel free to drop by and—"

"I'm going to have to move on, Mom." Wobbling moderately, Gates got to his feet. "My hideout here isn't safe any longer."

"Sit." She nudged him back down with a plump elbow. "Nobody else knows you're here except this housebreaker. So all we have to do, Shelly, is work out a foolproof way to silence him."

"No, that's not a good idea at all," argued her son. "Killing people isn't part of my—"

"We don't kill him," she told him. "We just toss him in a storeroom for a while. We'll feed him now and then and make sure that—"

"The Cosmos Detective Agency, a large and powerful, not to mention easy to get ticked off, organization, knows I'm up here in New Hollywood, folks," Gomez pointed out. "They know for whom I was hunting and they, in turn, will come hunting for me before I've spent very long starving in your storerooms."

"Mom, it'll be a lot simpler if I simply pack up and go someplace else to—"

"Oof," said Madame Sonja. She suddenly rose up on tiptoe, let go of her left hand lazgun and then the right. Dropping to her knees with an echoing thunk, she teetered and then fell forward onto the carpeting.

"Mom!" Gates knelt beside her.

Gomez was gazing toward the open doorway. He'd been the only one who'd noticed the hand with the stungun that had appeared there to fire at Madame Sonja while she was preoccupied in arguing with her suntanned son.

"Honestly, Gomez, it's an absolute wonder to me that you've survived in this world anywhere near as long as you have. I know you got me out of a jam earlier, but you most times, honestly, seem incapable of taking care of yourself or—"

"How did you happen to drop by here, Nat?"

The redhaired reporter came into the room. "Knowing you for an ingrate, I wasn't exactly expecting a hug and a heartfelt thank-you for saving your miserable neck, yet I—"

"Thanks. Now how did you find me?"

"By following the signal being given off by that tiny mike I planted on your coat when we parted," Natalie explained. "You're really, you know, so transparent when you attempt to be cunning. I sensed at once, and I would have even were I not the crackerjack reporter that I am, since you're that obvious when you attempt to be sneaky, that you were onto something big. I realized that this could well be the important yarn I need to save my own stymied career and get it out of the doldrums of show-business reportage so that—"

"An interview with Carlos Taffy, *chiquita,* would serve the same purpose."

"That doink? A conversation with him is just more pap for the halfwits who follow the dreadful tripe I've been forced to purvey." She shook her head, then laughed. "But this, Gomez—inside info on the Alicia Bower vanishment, this is a real story."

"I'm not too pleased," mentioned Gates as he rose up and glared over at her, "to witness you standing around smirking moments after felling my poor dear mother. It smacks of the kind of callous behavior that the media these days is all too—"

"Oh, stop your jabbering." She swung the stungun toward him and fired.

"Oof." The stunned fugitive stiffened, flapped his arms once and then fell over atop his sprawled mother.

Nodding with satisfaction, Natalie said, "Look around for something to carry him off in—a sack hopefully."

"Why do we want to pack Shelly, *cara?*"

"Because we're taking him back to Greater LA in my Newz shuttle," she answered. "He's, which should be obvious even to you, essential to my story. If I don't miss my guess this'll win me back my former high position in the broadcast sphere. 'Daredevil reporter captures fugitive. Comes close to solving heiress mystery.' " She smiled, nodding positively. "Oh, and if it's not imposing on you, and keep in mind I just now pretty much saved your worthless life, Gomez, I'd appreciate it if you'd shoot a couple of minutes of vidfootage of my standing over this fellow. I've found that this sort of obvious shot, involving the commentator in the action as it were, impresses the rubes and adds a whole heck of a lot to the impact of a news story. I left my vidcam hidden out in the hedge. Wait here while I fetch it, will you?"

"We don't really have time for a photo session. We ought to be—"

"Of course we do," she told him.

31

THE PIRATE MUSEUM was housed in an imitation galleon that was anchored in one of the Venice Sector's old canals. The museum had suspended operations nearly a year ago, and the canal had been dry quite a bit longer than that. The night wind was worrying dry leaves along the cracked canal bottom as Dr. Harry Moreno led Molly and Dan up the rickety gangplank toward the museum deck.

Watching them from the railing was a thickbearded pirate, who had a faded bandana over his shaggy head and a black patch masking one eye. "Welcome aboard, mates," he called.

The psychiatrist nodded at the android pirate when he reached the deck. "Salinas around?"

"Aye, you can bet your barnacles he is, Doc." The mechanical man jerked a thumb in the direction of a nearby lighted cabin.

"Salinas has been watchman here," explained Moreno, "ever since the place shut down."

The cabin door swung open with a creak. A lanky, weathered man of about thirty-five emerged. He had a scruffy beard and wore a battered Brazil War army jacket. He spoke out of a small black voxbox planted in his throat. "Dr. Moreno, hey, it's good to see you."

"Same here, Salinas." The men exchanged hugs. "This is Molly Fine and Dan Cardigan, friends of mine."

Salinas hugged each of them in turn. "Welcome aboard," he said.

Dan told him, "We're looking for Jimalla Keefer."

Taking a slow step back, Salinas eyed the doctor. "I take it you vouch for them?"

"Sure, and it's very important that we find Jimalla," he answered. "Is she here?"

Salinas nodded. "Down in the Pirates' Den," he said. "Pretty damn scared she is, too, but I can't get her to tell me what exactly's wrong."

"Somebody's hunting for her," said Molly. "Somebody who probably wants to keep her quiet about something she seems to know."

"I figured that," said the watchman. "Jim usually only drops in on me when she's in one kind of trouble or another—but I guess you know that, Doc."

"Yeah, this is the third of her haunts we've come looking for her at. Nobody's hurt her so far?"

"No, she's in okay shape, no bumps or bruises," said Salinas. "C'mon, I'll take you to her."

The Pirates' Den resembled a cave. Piled up against

one wall were treasure chests spilling over with glittering loot, golden coins, strings of fat pearls, silver brooches encrusted with rubies and emeralds. At a thick oaken table at the cavern's center five husky pirates sat stiffly and silently, their gruff bewhiskered faces illuminated by a flickering candle thrust in a dusty rum bottle.

The sixth chair was occupied by a thin black girl.

She jumped to her feet as Salinas crossed the simulated stone threshold. "What's wrong?" she asked, backing in the direction of the treasure chests.

"Nothing, Jim, everything's fine," he assured her. "Doc Moreno's looking for you, is all."

She saw Moreno and came hurrying over to him. She caught hold of both his hands. "Harry," she said very softly, "I think I'm in some new, really serious trouble."

"I think so, too, Jimalla." He put a big arm around her narrow shoulders and, gently, turned her to face Dan and Molly. "But these two, I'm pretty sure, are going to be able to help you."

"Well, if you'll allow me to give you my honest opinion," said Natalie, "he certainly doesn't look especially comfortable."

"Nat, the *pendejo* is still unconscious. Comfort isn't a concern."

"Well, I happen to feel that there's a code of conduct concerning these things, similar, I imagine, to how you're supposed to treat prisoners of war. What I mean is, you shouldn't throw them on the floor of your shuttle cabin like a sack of old potatoes."

"You're the one, *chica,* who suggested stuffing Shel in that plastisack in the first place."

"It would be much better, and more humane as well, it seems to me, if you'd at least put a pillow under his head."

"Carumba," observed Gomez, unbuckling himself from the passenger seat.

The official Newz, Inc. shuttle had departed the New Hollywood satellite nine minutes earlier and, with Natalie at the controls, was now en route for the Greater Los Angeles Spaceport.

Muttering, Gomez skirted the sack on the floor and took a cushion off one of the other passenger seats. He genuflected and arranged it under one end of the green sack that held the stungunned Sheldon Gates. "That ought to make him sufficiently comfy."

"Wrong end."

"Que?"

"You stuck the cushion under his feet."

"No, that's his head."

"Don't think I'm being critical of your judgment, though it's not all that good under the best of circumstances, but you can see his ears poking at the sacking down there at the opposite end."

Grunting, Gomez squatted and poked at the sacked fugitive. "Seems you're right, Nat. His nose does seem to be down here." Shifting the cushion, he plumped it and returned to his chair.

"Now, if you'll excuse me, I'll contact the head office of Newz and tell those dimwits about this enormous scoop that I've come up with. They're going to—"

"*Momentito,* Nat," put in the detective. "The fact that Alicia Bower is missing hasn't been made public yet."

"That's precisely why it makes such a terrific—"

"If you reveal that fact, along with the news that Jake and I are involved, it could screw up our chances of finding her."

"How?"

"In numerous ways."

"That is, which even you ought to be able to see, not a very persuasive—"

"It's standard procedure in a kidnapping, *chica,* to keep the news quiet for as long as possible."

"Is that what this is? Do you guys have evidence that she was abducted?"

"Not solid evidence, no. But we're convinced the lady didn't disappear of her own free will."

"Do you have any idea who snatched her then?"

"There are a lot of angles to this. Right now it's just not a good idea to broadcast the—"

"Hey, of course!" She snapped her fingers. "I've been hearing rumors for over a year about a possible link between Mechanix International and some sneaky government intelligence agencies." She watched Gomez's face as she continued. "Obviously those rumors are true, of course, and this hapless heiress somehow got caught up in some dangerous spillover from that. You may as well, you know, provide me with all the details, since I'm bound to—"

"Attend to me, *amiguita,*" he said. "There are several possible governmental trickeries tied in with this one. And, if you'll play along with me, I will, you have my solemn word, tell you everything just as soon as—"

"Your word, solemn or otherwise, usually isn't worth, if you'll pardon the vulgarism, diddly, Gomez."

"Cross my heart," he vowed, crossing his heart. "Give us a couple days before you break the Alicia angle. If we haven't found her by then, you—"

"And what am I supposed to do with Sheldon Gates in the meantime? Leave him in the sack?"

"You can turn him over to the SoCal cops," he told her. "Shel's wanted in connection with the murder of Ford Jaspers. The law doesn't know that has anything to do with Alicia."

"But, based on what I was able to overhear of your conversation with him, the acting CEO of Mechanix is the actual killer. Once Sheldon talks and links her to the killing, everything is likely to come out."

"Shel is a very evasive lad. It'll take a couple days at least for the cops to persuade him to tell them much of anything at all."

Natalie was thoughtful for a moment. "Okay, I guess apprehending a murder suspect is a big enough story to impress my tyrannical bosses," she decided. "Then, when I spring the Alicia Bower angle on them, it'll knock them on their collective fannies."

"Without a doubt," he agreed.

"If only," she said, glancing at him once again, "I could get over the idea that you're still conning me."

32

IT WAS NEARLY midnight and there was relatively little traffic to be seen outside the windows of Walt Bascom's tower office at the Cosmos building, mostly cruising brightlit skycabs. The agency chief was sitting on the edge of the desk, one leg slowly swinging, idly fingering the keys of his saxophone and watching Jimalla.

She sat, very straight, hands folded in her narrow lap, in a red plastiglass chair a few feet from him. "I'm still," she was telling him, "sort of afraid."

"We can put you up someplace safe for awhile," Bascom assured her. "We'll let your parents know that we'll—"

"I don't have much in the way of parents," she said, glancing toward Dr. Moreno, who was gazing out a window across the office. "Just my dad and he doesn't much give a darn where I am."

"We'll notify him anyway. But he won't know exactly where you are. Okay?"

"Yeah, that'd be fine, sure."

"Soon as she told us what she knew, I figured you ought to know," said Dan. "Well, no, actually, I thought I should tell my dad, but I don't know how to contact him, so I settled for you, Mr. Bascom. He's okay, isn't he?"

"At last report."

"But he hasn't found Alicia Bower yet?"

"No, not so far as we know."

Molly leaned over in her chair to tap Jimalla on the arm. "You can tell him what you told us."

"Guess I might as well." She lifted her hands off her lap, rubbed at her knees, refolded her hands. "I got to know most of the people in our therapy group. Not exactly as friends, but I know them."

Dr. Moreno turned his back to the window and gave the girl an encouraging nod.

Jimalla continued, "I never much liked Guy Woodruff, but—"

"Guy Woodruff, huh?" Bascom tapped the side of his saxophone with his forefinger. "We know him by another name, but go ahead."

"Well, I used to run into him around Venice pretty often. This one night I was at Kaminsky's Kafe—you know the place, Harry."

"A dump," supplied Moreno.

"Yeah, it is, sort of. I was in a booth with a friend and I heard somebody talking in the next booth to ours. Couldn't see them, but I recognized Guy's voice. He was talking with an old man, somebody sixty or so. Except this man kept calling him Sheldon and not Guy—well, that fits in with what you just said, doesn't it? Anyway, this old man was saying that somebody named Myra wasn't pleased with Sheldon's reports. Did he think they were paying him for a lot of drivel and no facts? He said that Sheldon had to put down every damn word that Alicia said in the sessions. 'You put it down word for word, Sheldon, and let us do the editing.' Something like that, is what the old man told him." Jimalla unfolded her hands, flexed her thin fingers and rubbed at her knees again. "I got, you know, curious. So I took a careful walk to the bathroom. They didn't get a look at me, but I saw them both. It was Guy for certain, sitting there with a thin, welldressed man who didn't look too healthy."

"You didn't hear the other man's name?" asked Bascom.

She gave a negative shake of her head. "And I just forgot all about it for awhile. But then Alicia disappeared and I got to wondering," she told him. "When Guy, or whoever he is, went missing, too, I knew something was going on wrong. Then I . . . well, I guess this was stupid, considering. I told a few people what I knew, even though I'm not exactly sure what it is I really do know. Next day, when I was about to go into the place I was staying, a couple of guys tried to grab me and drag me into their landcar. I kneed one and got away from them both, but I was really scared. I told my friend, Norm Porter, about all of it." She glanced at Molly. "Molly told me that some guys worked Norm over to get him to tell them where they could find me. That's even scarier."

Dan said, "I figured you could use the ID Simulator, Mr. Bascom. Then you could use Jimalla's description of that older man to maybe get an identification of him."

"Yep, we ought to be able to do that." The agency head moved closer to her and held out his hand. "Come on over to the gadget, child, and we'll give it a try."

33

THE MENTOR PSYCH Centre loomed up across the Staff Landing Area, a multistoried, blankfaced building standing grey in the grey morning.

"His electropass got us onto the lot," observed Georgia as her skycar set down on the grey surface of the lot. "So the other stuff Dr. Winter lent you ought to work, too."

Unbuckling, Jake said, "Getting inside is not going to be our major problem."

"No guards outside the Staff Entrance, just like Winter said." She left the car.

"But considerable awaiting inside."

They walked confidently across the early morning ground level landing area. At the opaque plastiglass door to the Staff Wing, Jake inserted the electrokey that the psychiatrist had given him.

Fifteen seconds passed.

Then, with a faint hissing sound, the door slid aside.

The initial length of grey corridor was blank, without a single door or window. Just before they reached its end, they halted.

Jake picked up Georgia and carried her in his arms. After one small laugh, she shut her eyes and feigned unconsciousness.

Around the bend in the corridor was a wide door labeled CONTROL/MONITORING #1. Stationed directly in front of it, arms folded across his massive chest, stood a large grey guardbot.

He turned his head toward the pair, asking, "What are you doing in this area, please?"

"Look—where's Dr. Cohen's office?" asked Jake in a very agitated voice.

"This section of the Centre is restricted to staff only, sir."

"I know, but Cohen's on staff, isn't he?" Jake moved up closer to the robot.

"If you wish to see Dr. Cohen—which Dr. Cohen is that, by the way? We have two on staff and—"

"Stanley," said Jake. "Listen, the medication he gave my wife—some kind of new stuff and if you ask me he shouldn't be handing out anything that dangerous to people— Well, I found her on the bathroom floor this morning. It's Dr. Cohen's—that's Dr. Stanley Cohen's—fault and we—"

"Sir, you should have called MedAlert and not—awk."

Georgia had swung up her left hand and slapped a

tiny parasite control-disc to the preoccupied guardbot's side. "Okay, you can put me on my feet now, Jake."

He did that, telling the controlled robot, "You'll let us into the Control Room. Understand?"

"Yes, sir."

"Far as you're concerned, everything is just fine. Nothing out of the ordinary is going on."

"Yes, sir."

The door slid open.

She had, she was fairly certain, lost some weight lately. It was hard to be sure because the plain grey dress they had given her to wear was several sizes too large anyway. She was still, too, having problems with her memory and she found she couldn't always keep track, when she tried to think back, of what she'd done during the day. Probably she'd missed some meals. Actually, she was nearly certain, she'd been losing weight even before she came here.

She wasn't even exactly sure how long she'd been here. A week probably, something around a week. Several days anyway. She knew where she was, though, she knew that much.

"And I know my name—it's Alicia Bower."

When she said her name, sitting there in the grey armchair, she felt a sharp pain in her side. That was something that had happened before and she had better ask Dr. Spearman about it.

Except, and she had no precise notion as to why, she didn't especially trust him. Didn't particularly like the man, even though he treated her cordially. Whenever the treatments that she needed were painful, he apologized and then explained that she'd had a serious breakdown. One that, unfortunately, sometimes required painful remedies. She'd be as good as new soon, that he guaranteed her.

The trouble was, Alicia wasn't at all sure how she'd felt when she was new or completely healthy.

She got up, very slowly and carefully, from the chair and took a few steps across the grey carpet. The grey slippers they'd given her didn't fit especially well either.

Yes, definitely she was thinner. She felt different when she walked, lighter and, somehow, much more vulnerable.

"I'll be like Slimjim soon," she said to herself.

That was odd, wasn't it?

She didn't actually know anyone by that name. Yet when she said that name to herself, very briefly, just for a few seconds, she had an image of a very thin black teenage girl.

If she trusted Dr. Spearman a little more than she did, maybe she'd ask him about things like that. Names and images that popped into her head. Names and images that, so far as she could tell, had no connection with anyone she knew or anything that had ever happened to her.

"Slimjim," she said again. "Jimalla."

Another image of the same girl and, for some reason, the ocean.

Yes, the Pacific at twilight. She was walking alongside Jimalla and they stopped to watch a robot, all trimmed in bright neon, juggling, his metal body framed by the glare of the setting sun.

Maybe when she was better, she'd be clearer about things.

The grey door in the grey wall slid open with that whispering sound it always made.

"Having a little exercise, Alicia?" It was Dr. Spearman, smiling in that way that was supposed to be friendly. He had the dark, thin medical kit tucked up under his arm.

"I want to ask you something."

The psychiatrist seated himself in one of the chairs at the round grey table near the center of the room. "Why, of course."

"How much did I weigh when I arrived here?"

"Are you worrying about that?"

"Not exactly worrying, but curious."

Spearman, smiling, stroked his blond beard with plump fingers. After placing the kit on the table, he took his phone out of a pocket of his medical jacket. He placed it a few inches from the kit, reached into another pocket. "We can certainly tell you that," he told her. He produced his handheld computer terminal. "According to our charts on you—119 pounds."

"And what do I weigh now?"

"Let's see—yesterday it was 115." He made a clucking noise, shaking his head. "I'm glad you pointed this out, Alicia. We'll, yes, have to do something about this."

"Not tubes," she said softly. "Please, I don't want to be fed with tubes again."

"We haven't done that, my dear."

"Not this time."

He set the computer aside, rested an elbow on the table. "You remember your earlier stay with us?"

"Some of it, yes. That was early last year."

Dr. Spearman nodded. "Well, I don't believe you'll have to do anything more than eat a little more at each meal," he said. "The nurse tells me that—"

"Was she my nurse when I had to stay at the Centre before?"

"She's a robot, my dear. They all look very much—"

"It's only that I have the feeling that there's something familiar about—"

"What have I been telling you about your habit of interrupting, Alicia? It's not an admirable habit."

She returned to the grey armchair and sat down. "I'm sorry."

"Come, sit over here at the table."

Sighing, the young woman got up again. She crossed to the table and took the chair the farthest from Dr. Spearman.

He said, "You also have to work at masking your negative feelings somewhat better. I know you don't like some of our therapy techniques, but there's no need to scowl and make faces. Those are a little girl's way of—"

"Was I here before?"

"You're interrupting again."

"I'm sorry."

"We were just now discussing your last visit. Don't you remember that we were doing that, Alicia?"

"Of course, yes," she said. "I mean *before* that time. Years ago."

"No." He shook his head. "No, you've only been here twice."

"Don't you have to doublecheck that on your computer gadget?"

"I have an excellent memory, my dear," Dr. Spearman assured her. "Plus a deep interest in your case." He rubbed his fingertips across his bearded chin. "What gave you the idea that you'd been—"

"I don't know. It simply flashed into my mind."

He moved his kit an inch or so to the left. "When do you think that other visit might have been?"

"It was . . ." She spread her hands wide, looked up at the grey ceiling. "I don't know. I . . . I was much younger."

"You had a very happy childhood and adolescence, Alicia. We've talked about that a good deal," he reminded her. "There would have been no reason for your coming here when you were—"

"My mother died when I was fourteen. That wasn't a very happy event."

"No, certainly not, my dear. But, really, it didn't have any harmful—"

"That's not what other people think."

"What do other people think?"

"That I'm promiscuous, indiscriminate about men. That I sleep with anybody and everybody."

"Do you?"

"No, not exactly. Not anymore, but . . . I'm not sure about how I used to be."

Spearman lifted the lid of the black kit box. "I'd like to begin our session this morning with—"

"It's morning, is it?"

"Don't you know?"

"I'm sort of losing track of time somewhat," she admitted. "I'm not even really certain exactly how long I've been here at the Centre. How long has it been?"

"Not that very long, my dear." Smiling, he cleared his throat. "Right now another injection is called for, I'm afraid."

Moving her right hand to her upper left arm, she rubbed at it. "Isn't there some other—"

"We've gone over all this before, Alicia, and I've taken you into my confidence as to our methods here," he said, very patiently. "In order to get the best results, the most beneficial results for you, we have to use means that are sometimes—"

"If the results are so darn beneficial, why am I back here?"

"You suffered a relapse."

"I'm still fuzzy on the details of that."

"Yes, that's to be expected in cases such as yours," he assured her. "There are, no matter how hard we work at it nor how much hope we put into it, people who have setbacks now and then. Now I'll get this injection ready for you, my dear, and we'll—"

"Jesus, are you still sitting here on your fat ass spouting the usual bullshit?" The door had whispered open and Sam Trinity, wearing a copperplated hand this morning, had come striding in. "I told you last night that this has dragged on far too—"

"And I told you, expressly, never to come here."

Shrugging, the OCO agent settled into the chair next

to the young woman. "You're not looking too great, kid," he mentioned.

Alicia moved herself and the chair back from him. "Dr. Spearman, who is—"

"A colleague of mine," answered the doctor. "And one who is not, I assure you, authorized to sit in on our sessions together."

"I'm staying," said Trinity. "I want to see why it's taking you so frigging long to take care of a simple—"

"I can't allow that, Trinity."

"Hey, you got this all ass backwards, Isaac. It's *me* who tells *you* what goes on around this dump." He reached out with his metal hand, caught a leg of Alicia's chair and pulled it back to where it had been. "You're giving me the idea that you don't much like me, sweet," he said. "You do like me, don't you?"

"You'll have to leave us now," insisted Spearman, standing up. "I cannot continue this therapy if—"

"You want me to continue it for you, Isaac? Because, you know, I think I can sure as hell do a better job than you."

Dr. Spearman rubbed his hand over his whiskered cheek a few times, looking from Trinity to the young woman. "Very well," he said finally. "You can sit in, but you have to keep quiet and not interfere in any way."

"I'm just an interested observer. Okay, Isaac?"

Alicia slid her chair back again. "Dr. Spearman, I'd prefer, really, not to have anyone else here while we—"

"It doesn't matter a rat's ass what you prefer, sweet," Trinity told her. He took hold of her arm this time and pulled her and the chair closer to him.

"Trinity, if you don't—"

All at once a loud hooting began in the corridor outside. Up above the door a band of scarlet light blossomed and began to throb.

From a voxbox beneath the flashing stripe of red light a message came booming. "Attention all security staff! Attention all security staff! Serious Rioting in Violent Wing! Serious Rioting in Violent Wing! Fire Raging! Fire Raging!"

Spearman took a step in the direction of the door. "I'll have to—"

The door slid open again. Jake, his stungun in his hand, came into the room. "Really isn't a riot, Dr. Spearman," he announced. "Just a little diversion I arranged when I was down in your Control Room."

"Who the devil are—"

"It's Cardigan, you asshole," exclaimed Trinity, popping to his feet. "And he's come to spring the damn girl."

34

"MISS BOWER, I'M Jake Cardigan—with the Cosmos Detective Agency in Greater LA," Jake said as the door shut behind him. "You're going to have to trust me. Barry Zangerly hired us to find—"

"You'll never pull this off, Cardigan," warned Trinity.

"Keep that hand in your lap, Sam," suggested Jake. "You, Spearman, don't go for your phone."

"This intrusion is absolutely—"

"Wait," said Alicia. "Why did Barry hire you?"

"Because you'd disappeared."

"That's absolute nonsense," said Dr. Spearman. "This young woman, Cardigan or whoever you are—this poor young woman suffered a serious relapse. To intrude here now and try to poison her mind with audacious and extremely harmful lies will only cause—"

"How'd I end up here then," she asked Jake, "if I didn't have another breakdown?"

"That was Sam's work. He's an agent with a government intelligence agency called the Office of Clandestine Operations," he told her. "Abduction is one of his specialties. I imagine he stungunned you when you went to visit your father in the hospital."

"You must, I insist, stop this," said Spearman, voice rising. "This girl's mental stability is not such that she can be subjected to—"

"If you'll just get up, Miss Bower, and come with me," Jake said. "We're on a pretty tight schedule."

She hesitated a few seconds, then rose to her feet. "Is Barry all right?"

"Relatively so. Some goons, probably in the employ of Sam here, worked him over."

"This man is lying," Spearman told her. "I don't know what his objective is, but if you go with him, you'll be doing yourself great harm. And you'll erase all the valuable work we—"

"This is no time for bullshit, Isaac." As Alicia passed in front of Trinity, he gave her a powerful shove with his metal hand.

That sent her stumbling across the room and smack into Jake.

Jake fell back, landing on one knee and dropping his stungun onto the grey carpeting.

Trinity lunged, shoving the fallen Alicia out of his way. He dived, landing on top of Jake and sending him over on his back.

"Now I'll take care of you," promised Trinity, his

metal fingers reaching for Jake's throat, "the way you should've been taken care of right off."

Georgia had headed for another part of the facility. Wearing a medical jacket and carrying a notebook, she went walking rapidly along a lemon-yellow corridor. She looked efficient, purposeful and as though she actually belonged there.

When the corridor forked, she headed down the sea-blue branch. Up ahead a few paces was a young human nurse, who was walking slowly alongside a robot breakfast cart.

"Damn," muttered Georgia, "witnesses." She increased her pace.

"No," the small, freckled nurse was telling the slowly rolling cart, "it's supposed to be *six* orders of imitation hashbrowns and *seven* of imitation homefries."

"On the contrary," said the cart out of its chromed voxbox, "it's *seven* hashbrowns and *six* homefries."

"That's absolutely and completely cockeyed, Oscar," said the nurse, her hands turning to fists. "I really don't understand why we have to go through this every single goshdarn—"

"Nurse, excuse me." Georgia had caught up with her and was tapping on her freckled arm.

"Oh, yes, Dr. . . . I'm afraid, since I'm new here, I don't know your name." She and the cart came to a stop.

"McClennan," said Georgia, smiling cordially. "Dr. Mary Lou McClennan."

"Well, what can I do for you, Dr. McClennan?"

"Nothing actually," answered Georgia, continuing to smile. "It's simply that I've been assigned to the Sharon Harker case and I'm going to her room now, which is just a few doors away. I didn't want you, or your cart, to become overly concerned if you saw me going in there."

The nurse blinked at her. "But we have strict orders that no one is to enter Room 314, Dr. McClennan," she said, frowning. "In fact, only . . . um . . . one person is allowed access."

"Yes, I know, Agent Trinity." She tried another smile. "I'm assisting as of this morning."

"I hope you won't think I'm being a stickler, Doctor," said the freckled nurse, "but I honestly think I should see some sort of identification or authorization before I just go on about the business of serving breakfast in this area. Because of the nature of this facility, as it was very carefully explained to me when I began work here two weeks ago, our security measures have to—"

"Shit, I would have to bump into a beancounter." Still smiling, she reached inside her medical jacket. "Okay, this should satisfy you, nurse." She snapped out a stungun. "Okay, please, go on into Room 314. You and Oscar both."

"Hey, I'm not allowed to violate our security rules," protested the robot cart.

"God damn, everybody got scruples hereabouts." She slapped a parasite disc on his polished chrome side. "Okay, Oscar, you roll your ass on down to the end of the corridor and wait."

"Yes, miss." The breakfast cart moved away.

"You won't get away with this," the nurse told Georgia.

"You got any notion what the hell I'm trying to get away with?"

"Well, no."

"Then quit being so critical," she suggested, reaching for the door handle.

Trinity got his coppery hand on Jake's throat and started to squeeze.

Jake swung up both his hands, gripping the agent's metal wrist. At the same time he brought up his knee and drove it into Trinity's groin with considerable force.

The redhaired man yelled with pain and his clutching copper fingers loosened their hold.

Jake pushed himself to his knees, still holding tight to the wrist.

Using Trinity's arm as a lever, he swung him to the right and hard into a grey wall.

The OCO agent hollered as he went slamming against the wall and there was a ratcheting, ripping sound.

He fell back and away from Jake.

But Jake was still holding the coppery hand. Its fingers were twitching and flexing.

Trinity went slumping to his knees. Shoulders hunched, he pressed his real hand to his empty sleeve. A wet red stain was swiftly growing on the cloth.

"I must get help." Dr. Spearman reached for the phone he'd set on the grey table.

"You'd better not." Alicia dived, grey skirt billowing, for the fallen stungun.

She snatched it up, sprang to her feet and turned the weapon on the psychiatrist.

"Now now, my dear, you're really not capable of doing me any harm." Spearman smiled at her and picked up his phone.

"Don't," she warned him.

"We'll talk about your feelings after I—" That was all he managed to say before the stunbeam from the gun hit him low in the ribs.

The phone spun up out of his hand, hit the table, bounced twice and then skidded over and fell to the grey floor.

Spearman's plump hands fluttered and he seemed to be trying to smile once more.

He tottered, sighed, fell over unconscious.

Jake, meantime, had slugged Trinity and laid him out near the doorway.

Alicia glanced over at Jake. "It would've been nicer," she remarked, "if you'd knocked him cold with his own fist."

"Poetic justice, but a mite too obvious." The alarms were still hooting out in the hallways. "We've got to leave."

She slipped the gun into the dress's only pocket. "I'm still not completely clear as to who you are," she admitted. "But I'd rather leave with you than stick here. So let's go."

35

THEY HEARD THE sound of running feet, a lot of them, both human and robot, over in one of the corridors that branched off the one they were hurrying along. The security people and other staffers were running toward the fake riot that Jake had created with the help of the Control Room.

"We only have a few more minutes before everybody realizes they've been flimflammed," said Jake as he and the young woman ran toward the Staff Landing Area.

"Did Barry really hire you?" she asked.

"He hired the agency I work for."

"What did you say its name was?"

"Cosmos Detective Agency."

"Oh, yes, I've heard of them." She was breathing hard from the running. "How badly is Barry hurt?"

"They beat him up, couple of thugs and a bot," said

Jake. "There was no serious damage, though, and he's recuperating well."

"In a hospital?"

"Last time I talked to him, yeah."

She said, "It's comforting to know he's still interested in me."

"Lots of people are interested in you, Miss Bower."

"Look, if we're going to be on the run together for awhile—just call me Alicia, will you?" she requested. "And your name was?"

"Jake Cardigan."

"That's right, you already told me that," she said. "I've been having all sorts of trouble remembering things."

"Understandable."

Stopping, she caught hold of his arm. "What do you mean? Do you know something about why—"

"We can discuss what I know after we get ourselves clear of this—"

"Oh, dear god," exclaimed Alicia. She was staring down the corridor.

A large matronly robot, gunmetal in color, was coming toward them.

"It's her," whispered the young woman, her grip on Jake's arm tightening. "It's Tin Lizzie."

The ball-headed robot on the small screen of the bedside phone said, "I'm sorry, sir, we're still not getting an answer."

"But there's nothing wrong with his phone?"

"Not a thing, from what the company computer tells us," replied the hospital switchboard robot.

"Okay, I'll try again later."

"Perhaps, Mr. Zangerly, you ought just to rest," suggested the roundheaded mechanism. "You tried your brother's home phone until our outgoing switchboard shut down at midnight, and then this morning, as soon as we were back on—"

"I'm anxious to talk to him."

"That's obvious, sir. Yet, since you're here to mend and get better, it—"

"Try his work number again," said Barry, who was propped up in bed and twisted toward the bedside vidphone.

"We did that very thing only—"

"Try it again."

"Very well, sir." The small rectangular phonescreen went blank.

"Where the hell is Rog?" Barry asked himself aloud.

The robot's image returned. "Roger Zangerly is not at Mechanix International," it announced. "As before, they have no idea where he is."

"Okay, thanks." He sighed out a breath, leaning back.

"I'm concerned about you, Mr. Zangerly." A handsome, blondhaired android physician had stepped into his room. He had his name tag, which identified him as an android, fastened to the pocket of his pale-blue medcoat.

"Who are you?"

"Dr. Malloy." He came over to the bed. "I'm filling in for Dr. Steinberg."

"What's wrong with him?"

Malloy chuckled. "Not a blessed thing," he answered.

"This is simply his day off." He seated himself on the edge of the bed. "I understand you're extremely upset about something and haven't been sleeping."

"I'm just trying to get in touch with my brother."

"It must be something extremely serious to cause you to—"

"Doctor, I appreciate your concern," Barry told the android. "This really, though, isn't any of your damn business, not at all. In fact, since I'm really feeling a lot better, I want to check out of your little establishment. Today—right now, this morning."

Malloy shook his blond head. "That's not possible."

"Sure, it is. I have the right to—"

"Not in your present condition," the doctor informed him. "You aren't well enough to—"

"What do you intend to do? Keep me from—"

"I hate to think that would be necessary," said Dr. Malloy. "But if you attempt to take a course of action that we feel is dangerous to your wellbeing, then we have a perfect right to restrain you in order to keep you from leaving the protection of the hospital."

"How—you going to tie me down?"

"Nothing that drastic, though you might be moved to a more secure portion of our hospital. It might even become necessary to administer drugs to calm you down, Mr. Zangerly."

After a few seconds, Barry nodded. "All right, okay," he said to the android physician. "That won't be necessary."

"For the present," said the android, "I'm also going to have your phone shut off."

* * *

The gunmetal robot was walking closer, staring directly at Alicia. "Just where do you think you're going, young lady?" she asked.

Alicia was still holding tightly to Jake's arm. "I haven't seen you this time," she said quietly, looking sideways at her. "And they've been trying to make me think you never existed."

"You're so addled, you poor thing, that you have no idea what's real and what isn't."

"No, I was right about you, dead right," insisted the young woman. "I remember you and— Yes, I remember what you helped them do to me the last times . . . the last time I was here."

"Well then, yes, we'll have to get you right back to Dr. Spearman again," said Tin Lizzie in her hollow, rumbling voice. "Stand aside, young man."

"Your perceptors need tuning." Jake grinned. "I'm not exactly a young man. Doesn't matter, since I'm not going to stand aside."

"Then I'll have to summon assistance to handle this situation." She raised a hand toward the panel built into her side.

"No!" Fumbling the stungun out of the pocket of her shapeless dress, Alicia clutched it with both hands and fired right at the approaching robot.

The beam struck Tin Lizzie square in the chest. She fought to get her metal fingers to the panel, but failed. Her arm swung down to her side.

When she hit the floor, facedown, there was a large rattling thud.

"Oh, dear Jesus," said Alicia, pain sounding in her voice, "I'm starting to remember things all over again."

He put an arm around her waist. "C'mon, or we'll miss our ride," he said as they started running again.

36

THE LITTLE BLOND boy continued to cry. Sharon Harker was holding him on her lap, hugging him, rocking gently in the fat, padded rocker. "It's okay, Sean, it's okay," she was saying. "We're safe."

"Want to go home."

"Soon," his mother promised him, "in a while."

"Want to see Pompom."

Sharon glanced over at Jake, who was standing near Alicia's chair. "I think he means you."

Grinning, Jake crossed the shadowy, windowless little room. "What's bothering you, Sean?"

The boy studied Jake's face, then scowled. "Not him. He's not Beepaw." He commenced crying again, louder now, eyes shut and mouth open. "I want Beepaw."

"We'll see Grandpa soon," she told him.

"Now. See him now!"

"Hush, Sean."

The door swung open and Georgia entered. "Jake, we got a skycar for you," she announced. "Be ready in about half hour."

"Maybe once we get home to Greater LA, things will—"

"There's something I want to talk about," Alicia said to him.

"Sure." He crouched beside her chair.

Georgia went over to Sharon and the boy. "He's still pissed off, huh?"

"They must have given him some shots at the Centre. Painful injections, some of them, and that's . . ."

"I've been thinking." Alicia took Jake's hand. "As best I can think with my addled brain."

"Don't let Tin Lizzie's judgment of you—"

"No, she's right." She rubbed, slowly, at her temple as she spoke. "I really haven't been thinking too clearly for quite awhile now."

"Spearman is noted for his ability to tamper with people's brains," he said. "One of the guy's specialties is erasing or altering memories."

"I'm sure, as sure as I can be of anything at the moment, that they did something like that to me," she continued. "When I was there last year, I mean. Then, after I started to remember again, somebody . . . Who was it who arranged this, do you know?"

"Sam Trinity and the OCO are involved. We aren't yet sure who else."

"The thing is, Jake, if I go home now I'm still going to have all sorts of problems," Alicia said. "I still don't know what exactly it is that people don't want me to know. Nor do I have the remotest idea who it is who wants me to forget. So I won't have any guarantee that they or somebody else won't just grab me and try all over again." She paused, running her tongue across her upper lip. "And there are much simpler and surer ways to keep people quiet. You can, for one thing, just kill them."

"All of that's true," he agreed.

"Suppose you don't deliver me home right away, Jake?"

"And instead?"

"Is there anywhere, anyplace you know of—a place where they can help me to remember?"

He thought for a few seconds before nodding. "I know of at least one, yeah," he answered. "It's not completely legit and doesn't exactly do business out in the open. It's hidden away up in New England and they specialize in what you need."

"Will you take me there?"

"You've been, it's obvious, handled very roughly by Trinity, Spearman and that gang," he said. "Reversing the process, correcting what was done to you and retrieving your memory—that can't help but be damned painful."

"Not as painful as being dragged back into Mentor, and nowhere near as bad as being silenced for good."

Jake said, "Okay, I'll make a call."

"Do you have to get permission from your agency before you can—"

"No, I'll handle this on my own," he said.

* * *

The twilight followed them as they flew eastward through the declining day. Five thousand feet below their skycar the lights of cities and towns were coming on.

Alicia, dressed now in the pullover and jeans that Georgia had dug up for her, was in the passenger seat, knees up and her arms locked around her legs. "You specialize in this sort of thing, don't you?"

Jake was in the pilot seat. "What sort of thing?"

"Finding lost and strayed women," she said. "Seems to me I saw something about you on the vidnews a few months back. You located somebody who'd disappeared. She was hiding out up on the Moon Colony and you brought her safely home. That was you, wasn't it?"

"Yeah, it was."

"What happened to her?"

"She's dead."

Alicia nodded her head slowly. "That may happen to me."

"Eventually it happens to everybody."

"You were in love with her," she stated.

"I was, yes."

"Does that happen much, your falling in love with the women you meet on cases?"

"You're safe."

"But are you? They must've told you about me," she said. "About my bad habits and all the many men I've slept with. If you marched them all by a single point, the parade would last for several—"

"Tell me, if you feel up to it, some more about Spearman and what went on."

"Do I make you feel uneasy, talking about my personal life?"

"Is that the effect you're trying for?"

She shrugged one shoulder. "This place you're delivering me to, these people—can they accomplish other things besides putting my memory back together?"

"Such as?"

"Oh, there are a few other problems I have," she told him. "After I met Barry, I changed some. I don't wander off much anymore. And I am, surprisingly, capable of being loyal."

Jake asked her, "When you found yourself at Mentor—did you know how you got there?"

"No, but Dr. Spearman explained that I'd suffered another breakdown. Apparently I'd started behaving very oddly and it was decided to send me there again."

"Was that why you went there before, a breakdown?"

She didn't reply for quite awhile. "That's the official explanation," she said slowly. "What Spearman *and* my father . . ." She planted her feet flat on the cabin floor, straightening up in the seat. "This is very rough to talk about. Because—because of the possibility that my father has been lying to me all along, too."

"You suspect that you didn't have a breakdown the other time either."

She gave a small, agreeing nod. "That's what I'm starting to think," Alicia admitted. "In some ways I want to be a good girl, to go along with the whole program and help Dr. Spearman cure me, rehabilitate me and all. Another part of me, though, held out. They really want me to forget something. Spearman, I'm certain, was using techniques on me that were supposed to wipe out parts of my memory." She paused, shaking her head. "It's so—if they succeed, damn it, then you even forget that they did something to you to make you forget. You can go around with a bunch of false memories of what your life has been."

Jake suggested, "That's probably enough about this for now."

"I remembered Tin Lizzie," she said. "I remembered that dreadful robot whom I wasn't supposed to remember. Something inside me, because I'm stubborn at heart, Jake, something fought not to forget. It's as though I were drowning and kept struggling back up to the surface. The trouble is, I can't seem to get completely out of the damn water and back on the shore." She glanced over at him. "How did she die?"

"They killed her," he answered quietly, "the Teklords."

"And you still feel, don't you, that you should've been able to stop them and save her life?"

"I feel that, sure, because I think I could've."

She said, "That's the same way I feel about preventing . . ." Her voice trailed off and a deep frown touched her forehead.

"Preventing what?"

"I can't remember," she said.

37

THEY CAUGHT UP with the storm while flying over the New York Sector of Tristate. Heavy rain started hitting at the skycar and crackles of brilliant lightning came slanting down across the dark sky.

Alicia, legs tucked under her, sat quietly in her seat, watching the storm deepen around them. Finally she asked him, "What's the name of this place you're taking me?"

"Doesn't have one," answered Jake.

"It's not called the National Screwball Foundation or the Home for Wayward Girls?"

"They prefer to do business very discreetly."

"Who runs it?"

"Lady named Maggie Pennoyer."

"A friend of yours?"

The skycar took a sudden bounce and lightning turned the wet darkness outside an intense pale blue.

Jake said, "A longtime friend."

"You really believe she can help me?"

"She's very good, especially with people whose minds have been tampered with in one way or another."

"What about the staff? Do I have to talk to another bunch of robots?"

"Last time I heard, Maggie had two humans and three androids working with her," he said. "Of course, that was about five years ago."

"Oh, that's something else I remember hearing about you. You were in prison—for a long time, wasn't it?"

"Four years."

"That's not so awfully long."

"Depends."

"It was the Freezer." She hugged herself, shivering. "That must be awful, being in suspended animation. Did you dream?"

"They tell you that you don't."

"But you did?"

"Some." They were over the Connecticut Sector of Tristate now and the storm wasn't yet as bad as it had been over New York. After scanning the dashpanel, Jake punched out a landing pattern. "We're going to a town called Bridgefield."

"I've been there. It was pretty dull."

Very gradually the skycar began its descent.

The lightsign hanging from the pole next to the rainswept landing area read NUTMEG NATURE PRESERVE.

"So it does have a name," observed Alicia.

"Camouflage."

The landing lights of their skycar swept across a stand of white maples while settling down to a landing on the nearly empty lot.

Jake got out, made his way around the car in the hardfalling rain and helped the young woman out. "We have to go up along that path yonder."

"How many acres does this cover?" She hunched her narrow shoulders as the rain hit her, moving close to him.

"About twenty."

The gravel pathway curved through woods. All at once on their right a sturdy oak quivered, then vanished with a faint sizzling pop.

"Oops," said Alicia, glancing around at the rainy night woods. "Is all this a projection?"

"Only about half," answered Jake. "It's a blend of real trees and holograms."

From up ahead came the sound of booted feet crunching on the wet gravel. A tall, lanky man, wrapped up in a plasticoat and carrying both a lantern and a tool kit, was coming down toward them.

Halting a few feet away, he held up the lantern and looked them over. "Howdy," he said at last.

"Evening," said Jake. "You must be Jason McNaughton."

"That I am. Maggie warned me to expect you folks."

Jake grinned.

Jason said, "Got some trees on the fritz. Want to fix them tonight, even though the weather is foul." He nodded curtly at Alicia, eased around her and continued on down the dark path.

"Caretaker," explained Jake.

At the path end was a clearing with a rustic cabin at its center. Yellow light showed at most of its leaded windows.

The realwood door came creaking open as Jake's foot touched the top porch step.

A small woman, not more than four feet high, was framed in the rectangle of light. "Jake, it's wonderful to see you again," she said, laughing.

"Same here, Maggie." He crouched on the welcome mat, put both arms around her.

Maggie Pennoyer hugged him, then kissed him on the cheek. "C'mon in and bring the injured dove," she invited. Her left leg was several inches shorter than her right and on her left foot she wore a built-up shoe.

"Maggie has the notion that I specialize in rescuing waifs and strays," explained Jake.

The stone fireplace and the logs burning in it were real.

Alicia held out her hand. "I'm Alicia Bower."

Shaking hands, Maggie told her, "You'll have noticed that I didn't turn out quite symmetrical. Some sort of manufacturing flaw. If I was one of those slick andies your pop turns out, they could have sent me back. Sit down, why don't you? Looks like they've been starving you."

Alicia took the indicated wood-and-leather chair near the fire. "I did that to myself, I think," she said. "Being in that place pretty much took away my appetite."

"Spearman." Maggie spit the name out. "Did you manage to coldcock that sadistic son of a bitch while you were extricating her, Jake?"

"Alicia took care of that."

Maggie slapped her right hand against her thigh. "Did you inflict considerable pain and suffering on him?"

"Just stungunned him."

"That's nowhere near what he deserves, the bastard, but it's, hell, a start."

"Jake tells me," began the young woman, "that you can maybe—"

"Got her calling you by your first name already, huh?" She smiled over at Jake. "What is it about you that bowls most women over? It can't be the fact that you're so battered and weatherbeaten, can't be the mean look in your eyes or the fact that you're almost always glowering. And that alleged grin of yours is so evil that it curdles the blood of infants and—"

"What say you concentrate on Alicia." Jake settled onto a raw wood bench.

"You're absolutely right, Jake. Besides, there's not enough time to fix all that ails you." She, limping slightly, walked over to the young woman and stood scrutinizing her.

"Can you—get rid of whatever damage Dr. Spearman did?"

"That's one of my specialties."

"How exactly did you get into this kind of—"

"Jake didn't fill you in, huh?" Maggie laughed once again. "Well, I used to be on *their* side. Yep, I worked for our enlightened United States Government for almost five years. During that time I came up with new and more efficient ways to erase harmful information from people's brains. I applied my system and, hell, there must still be several hundred poor doinks wandering around this country who can't think straight because of what I did to them back then. Then, about seven years ago, I suddenly came to my senses. Somewhat similar to a religious conversion, except I stayed a foulmouthed heathen. What I think I acquired, damn late in life, was a conscience. But, hell, most people never do manage to grow one. From that point, I've been devoting my efforts to reversing the sort of stuff I'd been doing."

"Doesn't that annoy your former bosses?"

She laughed. "Hell, it makes them chew nails and shit ingots," Maggie said. "I move around a lot, and so far they haven't caught up with me or been able to stop me. Do you like this latest setup, Jake?"

"Cozy."

"Jason comes with it—and he's about as much fun as my Uncle Si's pickled cadaver. But it's a nice quiet location and I've done some of my best work hereabouts."

Jake asked her, "How many other clients do you have in residence right now?"

She held up three fingers of her right hand. "Just three, times are a little tough," she said. "And the paltry fee I'm charging you, for old time's sake, isn't going to make me that much richer."

"But think of the satisfaction you'll get."

She nodded at Alicia. "C'mon, I'll show you down to your quarters," she invited. "After dinner, I want you to turn in. We'll start in the morning—*early.*"

38

BASCOM WAS PLAYING his saxophone when Gomez came into his office. Hazy morning sunshine was filling the big office and giving a fuzzy glow to all the clutter.

"How come you never play 'Cielito Lindo' on that dornick?" inquired Gomez.

"I've never found an acceptable bebop arrangement."

"My next question is—why'd you summon me here in the wee hours of the morn or thereabouts?"

"I heard from Jake."

"Muy bueno." Gomez started to smile, thought better of it and asked another question. "Is he alive and well?"

"His message was delivered by somebody else and I didn't speak to him directly," continued the agency head. "I talked with a very feisty attorney from Farmland. Georgia Petway by name."

"What'd she have to pass on?"

"Jake's found Alicia Bower."

"Chihuahua!" he exclaimed. "I assume she's okay?"

"Yes, and with Jake."

"And where the devil is Jake?"

Bascom rested his sax atop his desk. "Miss Petway doesn't know, mainly because he didn't tell her exactly where he was heading."

"But it's not our way?"

"Not yet, he told her that much."

Slumping into a canvas chair, Gomez put his booted feet up on a box of infodiscs. "Was Alicia actually within the confines of the Mentor joint?"

Bascom nodded. "Jake, with the capable assistance of Miss Petway, got her out of there yesterday," answered Bascom. "Dr. Spearman and our old chum, Sam Trinity, were temporarily incapacitated in the process."

"That's not good," observed Gomez. "Unless Trinity is under the sod, he'll be champing to get even with Jake for taking her away from him."

"No doubt," agreed the chief.

Gomez asked, "Does this legal *señorita* have any notion what this is all about?"

"Only that it looks like Spearman was trying to mindwipe Alicia. No word as yet on what it is everybody is so anxious to have her forget all about."

Steepling his fingers, Gomez rested his chin on them. "Possibly Jake transported her someplace where they can help her remember."

"That occurred to me."

"Could be it's Maggie Pennoyer's brain workshop."

"That, too, occurred to me," said Bascom. "And if we don't hear directly from Jake by nightfall, I may try to contact the lady."

"It might occur to that *cabron* Trinity to check with her, too."

"If he has any idea where she's hiding out these days."

Standing up, Gomez stretched and yawned. "We can't quite call this case closed, can we?"

"Too many loose ends," said Bascom, shaking his head. "Speaking of which, Sheldon Gates remains in police custody in connection with the murder of Ford Jaspers and he still hasn't said a darn thing. Meantime, I've got people monitoring the activities of both Myra Ettinger and Bernard Zangerly."

"Our client's *padre* is tangled up in this mess, huh?"

"According to the identification Jimalla Keefer helped us with, it's Dad who was one of the Mechanix gang in cahoots with Shel."

"I'm going to be checking with an informant later in the day, *jefe.*" Gomez wandered in the direction of the door. "Digging into Myra's links with government agents."

"Are you sharing anything with that redhaired reporter?"

"As little as possible," said Gomez.

The rain was still there in the morning, thinner and quieter now. After his solitary breakfast, Jake went out onto the cabin porch and sat in one of the raw wood chairs. Gripping his mug of nearcaf in both hands, he watched the rain falling down through the forest. Twice in the first fifteen minutes a tree shimmered and disappeared.

A little after ten Maggie came out onto the porch. "Good morning," she said as she pulled herself up into the chair next to him.

"How's it progressing down below?" he inquired.

"Moderately well." She rested her left hand on her left knee and swung her built-up shoe, slowly, back and forth.

"But?"

"I'd like you to come down and take a look at what we've got so far."

Jake studied her face. "Have you found out what it is she knows?"

"Yes, most of it," answered Maggie quietly.

"That's good, isn't it?"

"This young woman likes you, lord knows why," she told him. "More importantly, she trusts you."

"Maggie, what in the hell is bothering you?"

"Nothing, Jake my dear. Not a damn thing, not a single god damn thing," she said, gazing out at the woods. "I have an MD, don't I? That means I'm tough and I've cut up corpses that once were living, breathing human beings and I've watched cute little kids die. Hell, I'm a tough old broad."

"That's what all the polls show." Leaving his chair, he crouched beside hers. "You found out more than you expected."

"I found a hint of something."

"And you don't know whether you should tell her about it."

"Oh, hell, she'll have to know." Putting her hands on his shoulders, she got herself down out of the chair. "Have you wondered why I don't have any chairs built to my size around here?"

"I know the answer, Maggie. That would be too easy on you."

She nodded, laughing briefly and quietly. "Come along underground with me," she invited. "Alicia wants you to watch this, too."

39

THE FIRST UNDERGROUND room Maggie led him to contained two low white cots and an elaborate array of electronic equipment. Spread on a small metal table between the cots was what looked to be a collection of Tek gear.

"How do you use that junk in your work?" asked Jake when he noticed it.

"That's an adaptation of my own, not meant for Tekheads." Pulling herself up, she perched on the edge of a cot. She gestured with her right hand at the complex of equipment that filled the entire wall behind her. "By rigging a subject to all this formidable hardware—most of which is of my own design—I can get a pretty good idea of what's been done to their heads."

"And what have you found out about Alicia?"

"That clumsy bastard Spearman definitely tried to set up blocks to her remembering certain things," answered Maggie. "He's not especially deft, the damn butcher. On top of that, Alicia's pretty stubborn. The blockages didn't completely take, memories started spilling out and back into her consciousness. When people realized that, they got upset and decided on a return trip to that crackpot's facility."

Jake asked, "You know what they wanted to erase?"

"Not erase, Spearman's processes don't work that way," she corrected him. "Tried to block, hide, keep pushed down below the surface of recollection."

"But you know?"

"Yes, I unblocked it." She pointed at the scatter of Tek paraphernalia. "Now, by hooking a subject up to that and feeding the impulses into my own variation of an ID Simulator, I can produce what amounts to a holographic vidtape of what's being recalled inside the brain. These little peepshows aren't completely accurate, obviously. Since there's always a certain amount of subjective distortion and a loss of definition caused by the limitations of my equipment. But the results, Jake, ain't bad." In attempting to get herself to the floor, Maggie stumbled and fell to her knees.

Jake made no move to help her. "And that's what we're going to take a look at—the footage you got from Alicia?"

"Thanks." She got herself back to her feet by grabbing the frame of the cot and pulling. "Most folks would've rushed over and fussed over me. You know better."

"Could be I'm just heartless."

"Nope," she said, walking toward the door. "I've never had the opportunity of taking a close look inside your skull, but I've got a pretty good idea of what's in there."

Near the center of the large circular room four chairs were arranged on a low, narrow platform. Alicia, knees together and arms folded, was sitting in the leftmost chair. When Jake entered, she smiled fleetingly at him and nodded at the chair next to hers. "Sit by me during the show," she invited.

He took the indicated chair, touching her shoulder reassuringly as he settled down. "How you doing?"

"As well as can be expected," she answered quietly. "Did Maggie tell you what we dug up?"

"Nope."

Unfolding her arms, she reached out and took hold of his hand. "It's not very nice," she told him. "In fact . . . well, you'll see."

"You sure you want me to sit in on this?"

"Yes, I am. I'm going to need your help afterwards, Jake, because . . . well, you'll see."

Maggie had taken the rightmost chair and was holding a control pad in her right hand. "Shall we get rolling, kids?"

Alicia didn't immediately respond. Finally, very softly, she said, "Yes, fine."

The room lighting grew gradually dimmer and then darkness closed in all around them. Alicia pressed his hand tighter. Her fingers were chill.

A few feet in front of them blossomed a dimlit hallway. A pretty auburnhaired young woman, wearing a party gown, came in through the front doorway. It was late night outside this house.

"That's me," Alicia whispered close to his ear. "I apparently see myself as a lot cuter than I actually am."

All at once a door in the hallway was yanked full open. Standing in the rectangle of harsh, bright light was a younger, healthier Owen Bower. The wideshouldered man was wearing a short bathrobe and clutching a drink in his large hand. "Come here, damn it," he shouted in a gruff, drunken voice. "Come here when I call you or . . ."

Suddenly he was gone, the door was only open a few inches now.

"I don't know where that came from," Alicia whispered. "It's . . . out of context."

The other Alicia paused at the thin line of light, frowning, listening.

From out of the room drifted arguing voices.

"Don't try any patriotic shit on me, Treska," shouted Bower. "The price has already been settled."

"This has nothing to do with flagwaving, Owen. What I'm trying to tell you is that the Office of Clandestine Operations can't be bullied, certainly not by you or Myra, into—"

"Go to somebody else then."

"You know we can't possibly do that," said Treska. "Mechanix has a virtual monopoly on the sale of servomechs, androids and robots in Central and South America."

Bower gave a harsh chuckle. "You bet your skinny ass, Treska," he said. "And every name on this list of yours, from Antonio Corte on down, happens to be a customer of ours. If you want the people on this shitlist to have fatal accidents, then you'll have to work with me. And you'll pay the god damn price we agreed on."

"The price, Owen, *was* agreed on. But now you're attempting—"

"That was a tentative price. But the technical difficulties and the various arrangements have caused us to be more realistic," Bower told him. "To rig those robots and androids so that they'll arrange fatal accidents—believable fatalities that don't look anything alike—that takes time and skill."

"We won't advance you any further funds unless—"

"Quit screwing around with me. You know damn well you're going to pay exactly what I'm asking."

The projected Alicia walked slowly away from the door, disappearing into darkness.

"That was a year and a half ago, when I'd just come home from a date," she explained to Jake. "The door to his den wasn't quite shut and I heard them talking in there."

Another image grew out of the darkness. Alicia in jeans and a striped shirt, hair tied back, was standing next to a heavy wooden desk. In her hand she was holding a sheet of pale-blue paper.

"Darling, that's the list, isn't it?" Bower had come walking quietly into his den. He was older than he'd been in the earlier glimpse of him, wearing a grey business suit and not yet showing any signs of illness.

"You . . . you're going to kill these people." The paper was shaking slightly in her hand. "Every one of them, ten people."

"Ten unimportant people," said her father. "Oh, important to the OCO and to the Tek cartels they're in on this with, but not people who have much real value to the world at all."

"You can actually modify our robots and androids to kill people?"

"Easiest thing in the world, darling." Very gently, he took the list from between her fingers.

"And they'll fix it to look like an accident, a series of accidents?"

"We don't want anyone to get caught or arrested. We're not talking about kamikaze assassins here."

"I just don't understand how you—"

"Alicia, I'm really afraid you're going to have to go away for a rest."

The images were replaced by darkness.

Slowly the circular room grew light again.

"I can remember all the names on the list," said Alicia quietly. "Three of them are still alive."

40

ALONE IN HIS room, shoulders slightly hunched, Jake sat facing the tap-proof vidphone. On the small screen showed the face of his partner.

Gomez and Jake had just finished filling each other in on what they knew about the case.

"The problem is," Jake was saying, "that we can't prove much of this."

"There are still some *hombres* scheduled to get knocked off in the next few weeks unless this information gets spread around hither and yon," said Gomez out in Greater LA. "As I told you, I'm on the brink of being able to establish that Myra's in cahoots with some OCO boys. And, if and when Sheldon Gates tells all, that'll link her with a murder."

"That's only part of the mess." Then, grinning, Jake sat up in his chair. "Whoa now. Here's our answer, Sid—Natalie Dent."

Gomez tugged at his moustache. "I'm afraid, *amigo,* to ask you what the question is."

"This is the big story she's been waiting for," explained Jake. "She's not bound by the same rules that we are and, if I know Newz, Inc., they'll be overjoyed to have her go on the air right away and *allege* this whole damn conspiracy. She can give out the list, those that have already been assassinated and those that are about to be. She can even hint that Mechanix International is strongly involved."

Gomez said, "That would mean I'll actually be giving the *señorita* the sensational scoop I've been promising her."

"Once this is out, they won't go ahead with the killings."

"*Sí,* and Shel may be persuaded to break his vow of silence," he said, brightening. "And Bascom'll be in a better position to spread the word to some of his highplaced government cronies."

"I'll be staying here one more day, so don't give out anything on where Alicia is," Jake told him. "But go ahead with the rest."

"*Bueno,*" said Gomez, "it's as good as done."

The pretty blonde android private secretary rose up from behind her desk, placed both hands palms down on her desk top and glared reprovingly at him. "You've caused your poor father considerable anguish and worry, Mr. Zangerly."

"Yes, I imagine so," said Barry. "And it's not, I'm afraid, over yet."

The door of his father's office slid open. "You shouldn't have come here," Bernard told him from the doorway.

"Do we talk out here or in your office?"

"Allright, since you're here—come in. No calls, Irene."

"I'd give him a good talking to, Mr. Zangerly," said the pretty android. "Disappearing from the hospital, getting in a fight with an intern and then—"

"Yes, yes, Irene." The door slid shut as soon as Barry was inside the large, stark office with him. "Everyone knows you're here, our security system being what it is. That could be . . ." He sighed and went over to his desk.

"Dangerous?"

"I was going to say embarrassing." The gaunt man sank down into his chair.

"Where's Rog?"

"I don't know." He concentrated on arranging a stack of infodiscs that sat next to his voxclock.

Leaning, Barry swept the discs to the floor with the side of his hand. "Look at me. Look right at me, damn it, and tell me you don't know what's happened to him."

His father raised his head. "You and Roger have never been, not for years anyway, especially close," he said. "Why this sudden—"

"He was looking into what happened to Alicia," said Barry. "Mechanix is involved in her disappearance, and a guy named Rob Stinson and—and you, Dad. You're tied in with it, too."

"That's ridiculous. And, Barry, I won't continue this conversation if you keep yelling at me the way you—"

"Alicia is missing. Now Roger, too. I intend to keep yelling until—"

"Please, Barry, don't." He left his chair, knelt and started to gather up the scattered infodiscs. "What makes you think something's happened to your brother?"

"Because I can't locate him. I haven't been able to for two days."

"That's not unusual, he—"

"Roger's been checking in with me regularly. Then he stopped," his son told him. "Stopped in the middle of trying to find out what you did to Alicia. Have you had Roger killed?"

Bernard left the discs on the carpeting and got back into his chair. "He hasn't been hurt, son," he said in a faint, tired voice. "Neither has she."

Barry walked around the desk to stand over his father. "Jesus Christ, you've known all along where she is?"

"Please, don't shout at me," he said. "There's no reason why we can't—"

"Where is she? Just tell me where the hell she is."

The older man reached out, trying to take hold of his son's hand. "There are some things you have to under——"

"Tell me, you son of a bitch!" He yanked his hand out of his grasp.

"Over the years, Barry, you've never once wanted to listen to me when I tried to explain the financial reasons for my staying on here with—"

"Yeah, I know. It was your Mechanix earnings, your

huge impressive take, that put me through school and made me the respected academic I am today."

"It's only that . . . I got afraid that the money would stop. So I did certain things—"

"Don't! Don't try to blame your dishonesty on me," shouted his son. "I never asked you to finance me, you wanted to do it. I could've earned my tuition on my own."

"How?"

"You never quit, do you, even now? Maybe you thought I was lazy back then and couldn't have worked to . . . That's not important. What's important is you have to tell me where she is."

Leaning back in his chair, his father took a slow, wheezing breath. "We entered into an arrangement with a government intelligence agency," he began, his weary voice taking on a droning quality. "Owen set it up initially, suggested the whole idea to a friend of his in the Office of Clandestine Operations. It's possible, you see, to rig our more sophisticated mechanisms, program them to . . ." He paused, concentrating on breathing carefully in and out. "I didn't approve of it, but I found I wasn't up to going against Owen or Myra Ettinger."

"Program them how—to do what?"

His father's voice grew fainter. "In South America and Central America, you see, there were—"

"I can't catch what you're saying."

"The deaths in South America—I never quite got used to that," Bernard went on. "The OCO has relationships with certain Tek cartels down there and some of the profits are channeled into providing weapons for factions across Latin America, factions that the OCO approves of but can't openly support."

"Where do you and Mechanix fit in?"

"Owen and Myra and I, along with some OCO agents, worked out a way to modify certain of our robots and androids," the older man said, his voice still weak. "They could be used then to . . . well, you might say they served as assassins."

"Assassins—you mean you rigged them to explode like those kamikaze androids the Teklords use to kill each other?"

"No, nothing that crude, nothing so obvious and traceable," said Bernard. "But a robot butler, for example, could be rigged so that he would see to it that his master fell over a railing or drowned in the tub. A robot nurse might arrange things so that her patient seemed to have died during the night of natural—"

"What the hell does this have to do with Alicia?"

Bernard rested both his thin hands on his desk, linking the fingers. "She happened—it was purely by chance—to overhear her father talking to an OCO agent named Juri Treska. That was at their home. There was also a list of the proposed targets for—"

"That's what you call them? They're people."

"Alicia saw the list."

"It was just before she was sent to Mentor, wasn't it?"

His father nodded slowly. "Yes. There was no breakdown."

"And what did they do to her there—a mindwipe or some kind of surgery?"

"The OCO *and* Myra wanted simply to kill her. Owen and I—"

"Oh, yes, of course, yes. You're such a humane guy and her god damn father—sure, he loves her," said Barry loudly. "No, Owen Bower wouldn't let them hurt her. He'd just ship her off to that electronic bedlam and let them poke—"

"You have to understand, son, that Owen had to do something."

"No, I don't understand. He never had to let his mechanisms be used to kill people, he never had to let his own daughter—"

"Owen felt otherwise."

Barry asked evenly, "Is that where she is again—back at the Mentor Centre?"

"She was there."

"What do you mean?"

"It's confusing," said his father. "One of the OCO agents who was there was injured and . . . Myra suspects something has happened, though nobody at Mentor will admit it. She thinks Alicia escaped somehow."

"Then where is she?"

"We're not certain. There is the possibility she's still there."

Barry asked him, "What about Roger? Did they haul him off to—"

"No, he's here." He, very slowly, got to his feet. "We'll go find him."

41

MYRA ETTINGER WAS not pleased. "Bernard, you know how I feel about your barging into my office without—"

"It's too late," he told her.

She looked from him to his son. "You're not looking all that well, Barry," she said, lighting a fresh cigarette and exhaling smoke. "I'd say you left that hospital too soon and—"

"Where's Roger?"

"What makes you think that I—"

"Myra, drop it," said Bernard. "I told him."

She took another long, slow drag on the tobacco cigarette. "Told him what, dear heart?"

"Just about everything. I know you've got Roger held here in the Medical Wing, waiting until—"

"You damn idiot, there was no need to blurt out every god damned—" The vidphone beside her chair buzzed.

"Hold on, Bernard." She snatched up the instrument. "Yes—what?"

"Turn on the Newz channel," Juri Treska told her.

"Darling, I'm in the middle of an important conference and I really don't have time—"

"Just turn it on, you bitch." The phonescreen went blank.

Frowning, Myra poked a button on the arm of her chair.

The vidwall screen across the room came to life. There was Natalie Dent, sitting behind a realwood desk and looking directly at them. "These assassinations," she was saying, "the ones that have already taken place and those that are set for the upcoming weeks, were planned by the Office of Clandestine Operations and, we have strong reason to believe, also involved the active participation of several key executives of the powerful Mechanix International organization. Before I give you further details, let me repeat the list of victims and intended victims. They are Antonio Corte—"

"Well," said Myra after clicking off the wall. "This changes the situation, doesn't it?" Snuffing out her cigarette, she got up.

"It doesn't change a damn thing," said Barry. "You're still going to take us to Roger."

"No, not really," she said, laughing. "What I'm really going to do is get home as quickly as I can, pack a bag and head for a remote spot in Mexico. The bank accounts I've been building up across the border will—"

"Myra, you're going to do what we tell you." Bernard fumbled in his jacket pocket and got out a lazgun. "I don't need you to get Roger out, but I'll feel a lot safer if you come along with us."

She laughed again, shook her head, and started for the door. "I don't think, dear heart, that you have the balls to shoot me."

But he did.

Alicia caught up with Jake in the forest. He was sitting on a real log beside a simulated pond that was circled by projected pines.

Stopping a few feet from him, the young woman said, "We dredged up some more memories."

"So I heard."

The simulated leaves crackled realistically as she walked over to sit beside him. "Earlier stuff," she explained, "also obligingly blocked off by Dr. Spearman."

"You don't," he told her, "have to tell me about any—"

"But I want to—if you don't mind."

"Go ahead, sure."

After nearly a minute, Alicia continued. "I don't think I want to invite you to a screening of these new memories," she said. "I'm pretty quick, too much so maybe, at judging people. So I've already decided I can trust you."

"Trustworthy Jake Cardigan they call me."

Reaching over, she took hold of his hand. "After my mother died . . . my father started drinking a lot." She looked away from Jake toward the believable pond. "That turned him . . . well, nasty. He . . . um . . . hit me a couple times. But that's not what bothered me the most. It was . . . what he said to me." Her hand gripped his tighter. "What people say to you, people you love, that can hurt you a hell of a lot more than . . ." Pausing, she shook her head and started, quietly, to cry. "Jesus, I'm just sitting here babbling clichés. Sorry."

A real raccoon came waddling, very cautiously, out of the holographic woods. He halted on the far side of the pond, watching them with his bandit eyes.

Jake asked her, "What'd he say?"

"I was a wild kid," Alicia said. "Always getting in trouble at school . . . and a lot of other places. He told me, over and over, that . . . that I'd broken my mother's heart and made her so sick of me that . . . that she died."

"That's not what kills people."

"He said . . . he said that if they'd given him a choice . . . he'd sure as hell have been happier if I'd died and my mother had gone on living." Alicia bowed her head for a few seconds, sniffling. "After awhile, I guess I started agreeing with him. Eventually he quit the heavy drinking, but he never apologized. I . . . as I got older I must've figured if I couldn't please him . . . well, there were a lot of other men, especially older men, that I could please." She shook her head again, laughing briefly in a thin, sad way. "You're lucky, Jake, that you didn't know me back then. I'd probably have gone after you."

Jake said nothing.

"The first time he sent me to Spearman—I can remember now what he told me to justify that. He said it was because it was dangerous for me to know what they were planning. He, of course, trusted me, but the government people he was dealing with—he was afraid they'd kill me or lock me away somewhere. Because if I told what I knew, it would wreck their whole plan. So, because he loved me so deeply, he was sending me to Mentor to have them get rid of all the dangerous knowledge I'd accidentally picked up. Really, he swore to me, it was for my own good."

Jake said, "That was one of my father's favorite phrases."

She said, "My visit with Spearman convinced my father that Mentor was handy for potentially dangerous situations. That's why, when I started to remember again, he arranged for Sam Trinity to collect me for a return trip."

Jake asked, "Are you ready to go home?"

"Probably by tomorrow," she answered. "Now that, thanks to you and your friends at Newz, most of the story is out in the open— Nobody has any reason to try to keep me quiet."

"They'll be too busy covering their backsides."

She took his hand again. "I know I'm not your client officially," she said, "but can you do something, one more favor for me, Jake?"

"Probably. What do you need?"

"I'd like to go see my father, one last time this'll be. As soon as he's better, that is. Then I want to tell him, face to face, that I know what he did to me," she said. "That, I really think, ought to do me a lot of good."

"I can escort you to wherever he is, sure. But maybe Barry's the one who—"

"No, not him," she said. "This is a tough thing to say, since if it weren't for Barry, I'd still be locked away in Mentor and I wouldn't know any of what I know now. The thing is, well . . ." She shook her head. "I have to do some thinking about Barry and me and whether we're going to continue together. I'm not exactly, am I, the same person I was the last time he saw me?"

"Not exactly, no."

"That's why I'd like you to accompany me to this showdown and—"

Off in the woods hurrying footsteps sounded, leaves crackled and a twig snapped.

Jake jumped to his feet, yanking out his stungun.

"Take it easy, Jake," called Maggie. "Don't mow me down." She came limping into the clearing.

"Anything wrong?" he asked.

"In a way." She made her way up to them.

Across the simulated pond the raccoon turned away and went hurrying off.

Alicia slowly stood. "What is it, Maggie?"

"I thought I'd best come tell you," she said. "This just came over the vidnews. Your father died early this morning, Alicia. Natural causes."

Alicia lowered her head for a few seconds, then looked up at Jake. "He cheated me," she said to him. "Now I can't ever tell him that I knew."

He said, "What's important is that you know."

"And I'll have to go into mourning," she said. "Not for him, but for the man I thought he was."